By Mame Farrell

Marrying Malcolm Murgatroyd

Bradley and the Billboard

And Sometimes Why

and sometimes why

MAME FARRELL

and sometimes why

FARRAR STRAUS GIROUX
NEW YORK

Copyright © 2001 by Mame Farrell
All rights reserved
Distributed in Canada by Douglas & McIntyre Ltd.
Printed in the United States of America
Designed by Nancy Goldenberg
First edition, 2001
10 9 8 7 6 5 4 3 2 1

Library of Congress Cataloging-in-Publication Data
Farrell, Mame.
    And sometimes why / Mame Farrell.— 1st ed.
        p. cm.
    Summary: Eighth grader Jack is confused when he finds his relationship
changing with his best friend, an athletic girl named Chris who has suddenly
become attractive.
    ISBN 0-374-32289-9
    [1. Best friends—Fiction. 2. Friendship—Fiction.] I. Title.

PZ7.F2455 An 2001
[Fic]—dc21

                                                        00-49045

To my amazing, wonderful Shannon,
and to her director—my friend—
Tobi Silver,
who gives the gift of her genius
and nurtures dreams

and sometimes why

1

The ball hit the pavement with a wheezing thump.

"That's *S!*" said Chris, retrieving the ball as it bounced beneath the net. "All I need is *E* to win."

"No kidding." Jack scowled, and dragged an arm across his damp forehead. "I can spell, too, you know."

Chris laughed, taking no offense. "You're a crummy loser."

"And you're a rotten winner." Jack made a grab for the ball, but it evaded him, escaping through his opponent's legs.

For a while, there was nothing but the sound of sneakers sliding on blacktop, and the perfect, pounding rhythm of Chris's expert dribbling.

Jack gritted his teeth, trying to steal, trying to block. He lunged forward, shuffled back, reached for the ball again and again. But Chris—skinny, knobby-kneed, hair-always-in-the-eyes Chris—didn't lose control for a second.

Jack was getting desperate. "Traveling," he accused.

"Nice try." Chris grinned. "Now . . . gimme an *E*."

Jack found himself watching helplessly as the ball rose, from knees to waist to shoulders, only to be released from Chris's fingertips in a graceful arc toward the basket.

Swish!

Again, Chris laughed. "Always did love those vowels."

Jack had to smile at that, since it was an unmistakable reference to the day they'd met. Then he shook his head and crossed the driveway to lean hard against the garage door. It was the third game of HORSE Chris had beaten him at that afternoon. It didn't exactly bother Jack, since he had accepted long ago that Chris was the best basketball player he knew.

Best swimmer, too. And skater. Chris also beat him at tennis on a regular basis.

"Winner buys the sodas," said Chris, throwing a friendly punch to Jack's shoulder. "C'mon. I'll race you to the deli."

"Forget it." (Chris was also the fastest runner.) Jack

sighed, leaving the ball in the driveway and following his friend toward the cool shade of the sidewalk. "I just have one question. How do you manage to nail every shot with all that hair hanging in your eyes?"

"Concentration." Chris shook some rusty blond bangs aside. "Besides, my dad ordered me not to cut it."

Jack laughed. "All *my* dad ever does is yell at me *to* cut mine."

"Go figure, huh? I wonder if . . ."

But Jack didn't hear the rest of the sentence. Because at that moment, his pal Chris stepped into a patch of sunshine, and the light settled in Chris's bangs, making them shimmer above a pair of enormous amber-brown eyes, which Jack wondered if he'd ever *really* noticed before.

At that moment, Chris didn't look familiar to Jack.

At that moment, she actually looked pretty!

Christy Moffett was the first person Jack had met when he'd moved to Eastport; it was seven years ago, three months into the school year. He was the new kid in first grade.

Jack was assigned the seat across from Christy, and the teacher informed him that if he needed assistance with anything, Christy would be happy to help.

Christy, for her part, informed him that if he or anyone else ever dared call her Christy, she'd be happy to bash them over the head with her lunch box.

Jack had taken that to heart.

"Except if Kyle Baskin ever asks me to marry him," she'd confessed, her eyes dancing. "Only Kyle Baskin can call me Christy. If he wants."

Jack frowned slightly and glanced around the classroom. "Which one's Kyle Baskin?"

"Him." Chris used her pencil to point discreetly toward the back of the room. There was a dark-haired boy seated in the corner, with his back to the class. "The one in the time-out chair. It's his third time-out this week."

"Hmm." It seemed to Jack that a girl could do a heck of a lot better than a repeat offender like Baskin. But he decided not to say so.

The teacher returned, handing Jack a workbook. She told him they were finishing up the section on vowels. That information had put an immediate lump in his little throat; he could feel the tears pinching at the corners of his eyes. He'd left his last school when they were just *beginning* the section on vowels— he'd missed all of it there, and now, apparently, he'd missed all of it here, too.

Jack panicked. It seemed that he was doomed to go through life with no working knowledge of these mysterious letters. He would never learn the difference between short and long sounds, not to mention the whole silent *E* issue. His entire vowel-related education had been lost in transit!

One fat tear rolled down Jack's cheek.

"Oh, brother!"

Jack looked up from his empty workbook page into Christy's—make that *Chris's*—eyes.

"It's only vowels. It's not worth crying about."

"That's easy for you to say. You know them. And for all I know, you don't even need to." Jack lifted his chin. "I need to. I have one in my name. For all I know, you don't have any!"

Chris rolled her eyes. "I have vowels in my name, you nitwit. Everybody does."

"Oh." Jack lowered his head. "See. That's how much I know."

Chris said nothing for a moment, but Jack could hear the scratch of her pencil point. Seconds later, a scrap of paper came slipping across the desk toward him. She'd written "JACK."

"Which one?"

He blinked. "Which one what?"

"Which one's the vowel?"

Jack pointed to the letter *A* without a second's hesitation. "That one."

"See?" She surprised him with a smile. "You do know something about vowels. You know *A*'s one of them."

"Yeah!" Reluctantly Jack returned her smile. "How many are there?"

"Five. Well, actually . . . uh . . . six." She tapped her chin thoughtfully with the eraser end of her pencil. "No . . . five and a half."

Jack sighed. "I'm lost again."

"*A, E, I, O, U,*" Chris recited. "And sometimes *Y.*"

"Sometimes why?"

"Yeah."

Jack shook his head, frustrated. "Why what?"

"You mean why *Y*?"

Jack shrugged.

"Why not?"

"*Very* lost!"

Chris sighed. "Look," she said, snatching back the paper to write *A, E, I, O,* and *U.*

"That part I get."

She wrote another letter; Jack's eyes lit up with understanding.

"Oh!"

"Not *O. Y.*" Chris laughed.

So did Jack. "Now I get it."

"Good." She gave him a nod. "Nice work, Jack with an *A* in it."

"Thanks, Chris with an . . . ?"

"*I*."

"Chris with an *I* in it."

She'd glanced away for a second, toward the convict in the time-out chair, then turned back to whisper, "And sometimes *Y*."

It was their first secret, their first inside joke, the one that started it all.

Then the teacher was telling them to close their books and line up for recess.

And it was there on the playground that Jack's fate was sealed. The teacher told them to choose up sides for kick ball. Chris was one of the team captains.

She chose Kyle Baskin first.

She chose Jack Jordan second.

Being picked second, for the new guy on his first day, was just about the best thing that could happen to a kid, and Jack knew it.

2

They bought root beers at the deli on Main Street, then walked up two blocks to Hot Rollers, the salon where Chris's father worked. Through the window, they could see that his station was empty.

"Probably out to lunch," said Chris.

"With Soxie?"

"Probably." Chris grinned. "Stop drooling, Jack."

As they made their way along Main Street, the shops and restaurants began to thin out. Soon they'd reached the fence that marked the property of the Eastport Country Club.

It was a tall, black, iron fence. Every thirty feet or so, the bars were decorated with scrollwork crests bearing the club insignia. Cast in iron—permanent, indestructible.

From out here the whole place looked magical—the lush, manicured lawn, dotted with wicker furniture and shade trees, was merely a preamble to the golf course, a green expanse of swells and valleys that rolled on for acres. The tennis courts were situated at the top of a small hill, and below them the huge swimming pool rippled in the sunlight. At the center of it all stood the vast, Victorian clubhouse, with its covered verandas, gingerbread-decorated balconies, and turrets that rose into the blue brilliance of the sky.

It was Eastport's premier social establishment. It was the county's most exclusive club.

It was Jack's club.

A security guard stood by the open gate at the top of the driveway. He lifted one white-gloved hand to tip his cap as he nodded to Chris. "Well, hello there, young lady. And Master Jack Jordan. How're y'all this fine afternoon?"

Chris smiled. "Fine."

"Hi, Kirby," Jack said, then turned to Chris. "Wanna go in?"

Chris rolled her eyes. "Is it Bring a Guest from the Wrong Side of the Tracks Day?"

Kirby winked at her and chuckled. "She's a feisty one, yessir," he said. "My kind of girl."

Chris beamed at him.

"Don't encourage her," Jack joked. "She's already a big enough pain in my rear."

"Every young man should be so lucky!" pronounced Kirby with a nod.

This time, Jack rolled his eyes. "C'mon," he said to Chris. "We can play tennis."

"Without racquets?"

"Mine's in the pro shop. They've been restringing it. You can use the extra one my mom keeps in her locker."

Chris hesitated, but Jack knew she had no restraint when it came to playing tennis at the club. She couldn't resist the temptation of its meticulously maintained clay courts, which were such a contrast to the public ones at Randall Park, with their cracked pavement surface and sagging nets.

"Fine. Whatever."

Jack grinned as they started up the driveway to the clubhouse.

He led her inside to the door of the women's locker room, told her his mom's locker number and combination, and sent up a silent prayer that she wouldn't run into Emily Baskin or any of her stuck-up friends in there. Emily and Chris were your basic fire-and-gasoline combination and pretended not to know each other.

Minutes later, they were climbing the immaculate brick stairway to the tennis courts, where Jack retrieved his newly strung racquet from Charlie, the tennis pro, and signed up for the next available court.

"We're on deck," he told Chris, taking a seat at one of the courtside umbrella tables.

Chris settled into a green wrought-iron chair and surveyed the area, which was populated mostly by middle-aged women in vibrantly colored tennis outfits with coordinating sun visors and other accessories. The court nearest their table, however, was occupied by two guys who were a year or so older than Jack and Chris. Jack recognized one of them. Last year the guy had won every club tennis tournament in the fifteen-year-old division. Unlike Jack and Chris, who were going to be freshmen at Eastport High in the fall, Sam Templeton was a student at the all-boys Brenton Hall Academy; his gym bag, with its prestigious Brenton Hall crest emblazoned in white on the red nylon, was propped up against the fence.

Sam tossed the ball up and executed a Wimbledon-caliber serve.

"Who's he?" Chris asked.

"Sam something-or-other. He's pretty good."

"He looks good."

Jack turned to face her. "What's that supposed to mean?"

"It means," replied Chris, eyeing Jack strangely, "that he looks good. He looks like he plays a killer game of tennis." She poked him with the racquet. "Nitwit."

Jack pretended not to hear that last part. He had no idea why her statement had made him feel so wary.

They watched in silence for a while.

"Listen . . ." Jack began.

"Yeah?"

"I need a favor."

"Sure. What?"

Her willingness to help him made him feel even worse about asking. But he was desperate. "I need you to come to the Summer Cotillion with me."

"Cotillion?" Chris narrowed her eyes. "As in dance?" She nodded in the direction of the sprawling clubhouse beyond the courts. "As in *here*?"

"Yeah." He sighed. "I know you're, like, allergic to that kind of stuff, but . . ."

"You can't be serious."

"I am."

Chris groaned. "Me? At a country club dance? With Emily Baskin, God's Gift to Lip Gloss? And Davis Hastings Everett the Turd?"

"Yes. Davis Hastings Everett the *third*."

"And I suppose I'd have to wear a dress?"

This made him smile. "It won't kill you, you know."

"You don't know that for sure."

Jack laughed. "Yeah, I do. In the entire history of Western civilization, no one has ever died from having to wear a dress."

"Okay, so you wear one."

"That would be dumb."

"Not any dumber than *me* wearing one."

"Just think of it as . . . as a field hockey skirt, only fancier." He plucked at the strings of his racquet. "Amy will help you pick one out."

Amy was Jack's older sister. Her life revolved around two things: her wardrobe, and her Neanderthal of a boyfriend, Cuff.

Chris considered his suggestion, still skeptical. "They'd laugh me . . . they'd laugh *us* right off the—"

She stopped when a tennis ball sailed over the fence and bounced to a stop beneath their table. It was clearly the result of some lousy aim by Sam of the Super Serve, who was now jogging across the court toward them.

Jack found himself wondering why Chris hadn't just picked the ball up and thrown it back over the fence; she certainly had the arm for it. For that matter, he asked himself, why hadn't he?

She must have read his mind, because she was just

lifting the ball from the patio when Sam arrived at the fence. For a second, he stood there looking at Chris through the chain link with a strange, lopsided grin. She lobbed the ball up and over, and he backed up a few steps to catch it on the fly.

"Thanks." (Still grinning.)

"You're welcome."

(*Still* grinning.) "Haven't I seen you playing at Randall Park?"

"Um . . ." Chris was grinning now, too, as if the condition were contagious. "Maybe."

"Yeah. I watched you play last weekend." Sam shook his head in admiration. "You were awesome."

Chris thanked him, but it was little more than a whisper; if Jack didn't know better, he'd have thought she was blushing. It suddenly occurred to him that maybe Sam's aim hadn't been so poor after all. It might, in fact, have been dead on.

"Hey," said Sam, tossing the ball up and catching it. "Think maybe we could play sometime? Together, I mean."

Chris managed a nod. "Sure," she said. Actually, she kind of squeaked it.

Then Sam did something that was either the smoothest or the corniest thing Jack had ever witnessed. He reached into the gym bag for a pen, wrote something on the tennis ball, then tossed it back over the fence to Chris.

"Call me when you feel like a match."

Jack wondered if there was supposed to be some kind of a double meaning to that; if Chris noticed, though, she wasn't letting on.

"Okay," she said.

"See ya."

"See ya."

"See ya," said Jack, but neither of them seemed to hear it.

He and Chris watched as Sam returned to his game. Then two of the sun-visored women finished their set, freeing up a court. Jack practically sprang out of his chair. Chris was a little slower off the block.

As the women passed, they made a point of eyeing Chris's T-shirt and running shorts scornfully. One muttered something to her friend as she accepted a tall iced tea from the waiter, who'd seemed to appear magically at the edge of the patio the minute their game had ended.

For a moment, Jack wished he could take a swipe at the old biddies with his racquet. For another moment, he was afraid Chris might actually do it. But she didn't.

"I'll go," she said.

Jack stopped walking and looked at her. "To the cotillion?"

"Yeah. To the cotillion. It was *your* idea."

Jack nodded. "And you're gonna wear a dress?"

"Or a reasonable fascimile thereof." Chris smiled. "It won't kill me, you know."

No, thought Jack, sneaking a glance at Sam as they headed toward their court. But why do I suddenly have the feeling that it just might kill me?

3

On the way to Chris's house, she kept asking him if he thought it was a joke. She was bouncing her new tennis ball as they walked, and Jack found himself hoping the repeated contact with asphalt would rub off Sam's phone number.

No, he told her, as far as he could tell, Sam was serious about playing tennis with her.

Really?

Yes, really.

Are you sure?

Yes, I'm sure.

At the salon, Chris asked if he'd mind stopping while she said hello to her father. Jack said that was fine with him and followed her through the frosted double doors. The place was busy for a Tuesday.

Soxie spotted them. She smiled at Chris, then motioned toward a station in back where Mr. Moffett was highlighting a scrawny supermodel type.

As was customary, Chris dared Jack, in a whisper, to wink at Soxie.

As was also customary, Jack, in a whisper, told her to shut up.

He dropped his racquet onto the banquette in the waiting area and sat down. Chris made her way toward her father, leaned close to him, and said something in his ear. Mr. Moffett's eyebrows rose slightly and, when Chris showed him the tennis ball, he laughed and kissed her on the cheek. After that, he fussed with her bangs a little, and she rolled her eyes at him, then pointed to Jack in the waiting area. Mr. Moffett turned and gave Jack a little salute.

Jack waved back, watching as Mr. Moffett talked to Chris, all the while repeatedly dipping a skinny comb into some goop, applying it to a section of the scrawny girl's hair, then folding the hair into little squares of aluminum foil.

In a few minutes Jack and Chris left the salon. They headed into the alley that led to the rear parking lot, then up the steps to the Moffetts' apartment.

"Got anything to eat?" Jack asked, opening the refrigerator door and sticking his head in to investigate.

"Leftover fajitas for you," Chris told him, plugging in the blender. "Protein shake for me. Throw me that soy milk, will you? And the wheat germ."

"Here." Jack handed over the ingredients, then removed a plastic-wrapped platter of fajita fixings and a jar of salsa and shut the door.

Chris poured some soy milk and reached for the huge container of powdered drink mix that stood at the ready beside the blender.

"How can you drink that stuff?" asked Jack, arranging some strips of steak and chicken on a tortilla and popping it into the microwave.

"Well, first I pour it in a glass, then I bring the glass to my lips . . ."

"You know how they make that stuff, don't you?" He snatched the container and pretended to read the label. "They dig up the remains of great American athletes, grind their bones into powder, add some artificial color, and . . ."

Chris gasped. "That's disgusting!" Her eyes were wide open with horror. "*Artificial* color?"

They laughed over the sound of the whirring blender. When the shake was ready, she dunked her finger into the mixture and offered it playfully to Jack.

"C'mon, taste it."

He shook his head; Chris popped her finger into her own mouth, then pulled it out clean. "Mmmm."

"What's it taste like?"

"Babe Ruth."

"Says here the primary ingredient is seaweed."

"Okay—Babe Ruth after a day at the beach."

Jack removed the plate from the microwave, and dumped some salsa onto his fajita. He followed Chris into the living room, where they sat on the sofa and propped their feet up on the coffee table.

Chris was drinking straight from the blender container, which she held like a gigantic mug. Halfway through the shake, she stopped drinking.

Jack was licking some salsa that had dripped down his wrist. "What's wrong?"

"Nothing. I . . . I've just got a stomachache."

"That'll teach you to drink dead jocks."

But Chris was rubbing her abdomen. "It's not funny."

"Sorry." Jack put down his tortilla and became serious. "Are you okay? Should I get your dad?"

Chris shook her head. "No. I'm just gonna—"

Without finishing her sentence, she got up and headed for the bathroom. Jack watched her go, thinking that if she was going to throw up, he should probably go with her so he could hold her hair back or—

"Oh, my God."

"Chris?" Jack jumped up from the couch and was at the bathroom door in nothing flat. "What is it? What's wrong?"

Her voice through the door was muffled. "You're not going to believe this . . ."

"What?" He was beginning to panic. "Are you okay?"

"Yeah. I'm fine." Through the door, he couldn't hear anything.

"C'mon, Chris! You're scaring me here." His whole body was pressed against the door now, and his own stomach was beginning to churn. "What's going on?"

She drew in a deep breath. "Jack . . . I need your help. I need you to do me a favor."

"Sure." He leaned his forehead against the wood. "Anything."

"I need you to go to the drugstore . . . You've got to get me a box . . . of tampons."

"A box of crayons?"

"No, you nitwit! *Tampons.* You know. Feminine . . . stuff."

Jack sprang away from the door as if it were suddenly red hot. "You're kidding!"

"I wish." He heard her sigh. "I know this is weird, Jack. But it's my first . . . you know . . . my first . . . period. I don't have any of that stuff."

Jack squeezed his eyes shut and dropped his chin to his chest. The girl probably had a hundred Ace bandages lying around, who knew how many instant cold packs in the freezer, and at least three pairs of crutches under her bed—but the one crucial piece of health-related equipment she *really* had a use for right now . . . nowhere!

It was Jack's turn to breathe deep. "What kind?"

"I don't know!" she snapped. "You've seen the same TV ads I have. You figure it out!"

Whoa! He retreated a step farther from the door. Those mood swings didn't waste any time kicking in, did they?

"Jack?"

"Yes, Chris?"

"Sorry."

"It's okay."

"Maybe you should just go downstairs and ask my dad."

"*Bad* idea."

"What about Soxie?"

"Oh, no." He clenched and unclenched his hands. "I'll just . . . I'll run to the store. It's not a problem."

"Yes, it is."

He could hear the humor in her voice; it made him smile.

"Yeah, well, you'd do it for me. So . . . what kind?"

"Uh, I guess if they have, like, a beginner's model or something . . ."

"Right. Like Little League tampons."

"Jack! You're not making this any easier!"

"Sorry, sorry." He checked his pockets for cash. "Okay, I'm leaving now. I'll be right back."

"I'm not going anywhere" was her grumbled reply.

Jack took the stairs two at time; when he reached the alley behind Hot Rollers, he hooked left, toward Plum Street. McNeil's Pharmacy was about four doors up on Plum; he figured he'd have less chance of running into anyone he knew at McNeil's than at the big chain drugstore over on Main.

Inside McNeil's he was met by the familiar drugstore aroma of chocolate, antiseptic, and perfumed soaps. It took a moment to get his bearings, since he wasn't entirely sure where he was heading. He saw old Mrs. McNeil behind the counter; she seemed to be the only person in the store, so he relaxed a bit. Still, he wasn't taking any chances; he strolled through the relative safety of the cold remedy aisle and wasted a minute or two near the dental care display before finally making his move.

With his head low and his heart racing, Jack slipped into the feminine hygiene section. He half expected an alarm to sound, as if he were trespassing on private female ground. The sooner he got out of there the better, he decided. He forced himself to look at the shelves.

Well, he thought with a scowl, he had to say this for McNeil's—they certainly carried a variety. His eyes scanned the pink and powder blue packages quickly— slender, regular, superabsorbent. Deodorant, overnight, flushable . . .

He could feel the color creeping up the back of his neck as he examined a box of panty shields. What the heck were they for? Underwear engaged in hand-to-hand combat? And what was up with the wings?

"Can I help you?"

Jack froze.

"You look a little confused."

"A little," Jack grumbled. Actually, he'd reached the point at which he wouldn't have minded some assistance—anything to get this errand over with. It was just that he'd have appreciated it a whole lot more if the offer had come from kindly old Mrs. McNeil. And not from her son, Steve.

"I'm helping out a friend," Jack explained.

"Well, I didn't think they were for you!" Steve's hearty laugh rang through the pharmacy. Mrs. McNeil peered curiously around the cash register, but Steve gave her a capable nod. "Just another feminine protection rookie," he assured his mother. "It's under control."

When he turned his attention back to Jack, the guy was all business.

"Okay," he said crisply, nodding at the shelves. "You've got your two basic types of equipment here— the tampon variety, and the sanitary napkin variety. Both have their individual strengths, although tampons probably serve a much broader purpose for the active lifestyle of today's woman."

Jack stared at Steve in awe.

"Now," Steve continued, "the most important consideration, of course, is absorbency. There's regular absorbent, and superabsorbent. Needs will vary, partly based on the point during the menstrual cycle at which the purchase is being made. Do you happen to know the present needs of the female in question?"

What really amazed Jack was that Steve McNeil was able to say all of this with a straight face.

"She's . . . it's . . . today's her first day."

"First day this month?" Steve asked.

"First day ever," Jack managed.

"Ahhhhh." Steve stroked his chin pensively. "Well, that makes an enormous difference, as you might imagine."

Jack couldn't.

Steve reached out, chose a box labeled Slender Teen, and handed it to the rookie shopper.

Jack accepted the package gingerly. Well, Chris was

definitely a teen, but the slender bit confused him. "Do these have a weight requirement?"

Steve shook his head and explained the slender reference. If Jack could have disappeared into thin air, he would have.

"Get it?" Steve asked, sounding like a concerned math tutor.

"Yeah," muttered Jack. "I get it."

Then Steve took another package off the shelf. "Pads. Just in case."

Whatever that means, Jack thought. "Thanks."

"No problem. And good luck out there."

After Mrs. McNeil rang him up, she bagged his purchase and told him to come again.

Not if my life depended on it, Jack vowed silently.

He hurried down Plum Street, and in a few moments was running up the stairs to Chris's.

4

'm back," he called, approaching the bathroom door. "Uh . . . how do you want to do this?"

"Just open the door a little and hand it over," snapped Chris. "But turn your head."

Obediently, Jack did as she asked, keeping his head outside of the door while he reached in with his arm. He gave the bag a little toss, hoping it would land directly at Chris's feet, then he withdrew his arm and shut the door, fast!

It was quiet for a moment.

"How'd I do?"

"Fine. I think. I'll let you know in a minute."

He could hear paper tearing; he knew he should probably go back to the sofa and sit down, but he didn't. He wanted to be there, as strange as it sounded, for moral support.

"Does this, uh, period thing . . . hurt?"

"Not exactly . . . it's weird. It doesn't hurt, it just feels . . . different."

"What about the stomachache?" he asked, hearing the shiver of worry in his voice. "Is that normal?"

"I think so. You know . . . cramps."

Cramps! At last—familiar ground. Like shinsplints, and muscle pulls. "So maybe you can just walk it off . . ."

"Maybe." She laughed.

He waited a little longer but didn't say anything. After what seemed like a lifetime, he heard the toilet flush, and then the door opened.

Chris jumped. Jack jumped.

"All set?"

"I guess."

Jack's first instinct told him just to avoid eye contact, stare straight ahead. But what was that going to accomplish? Was he never going to look at her again?

Chris seemed equally uncomfortable, casting her eyes downward and fidgeting around.

Then he turned to her and smiled, figuring he looked as ridiculous as he felt, but she smiled, too, and looked pretty ridiculous herself.

The awkwardness was gone instantly. They made their way to the sofa and went back to their snacking.

"So you're okay with it, huh?"

Chris shrugged. "I don't have much of a choice, do I?"

Jack took a bite of his fajita, hesitated, then said, "Can I tell you something?"

"Sure."

"I thought you already had it. I mean, that you've been getting it. For a while."

Chris sipped her protein drink. "Well, I suppose you would have. I mean, most girls get it a lot earlier than this."

"When?" asked Jack, surprised by how curious he was, not to mention how easily they were discussing it.

"I don't know. Fifth grade, some. Sixth and seventh, probably, for most."

"Oh."

"I think it has something to do with sports—mine taking so long, I mean. I've heard that serious athletes, like Olympic gymnasts, sometimes don't get it until really late."

"This is gonna sound stupid but . . . why?"

"Why do jocks get it later?"

"Well, yeah, and just . . . why do girls get it at all?"

Chris looked at him like he'd just grown a second head. "You're kidding, aren't you?"

"Not really." Jack fell back into the sofa cushions and shrugged. "I know it has to do with becoming pregnant—or *not* becoming pregnant—or something. I was just never clear on the specifics. No big deal."

But it was a big deal. For some reason, Jack absolutely had to know—needed to know, to understand this whole issue. Because from the second Chris had stammered the news from the other side of the bathroom door, Jack had been feeling the strangest sense of loneliness. He'd felt as if that door had somehow become eight miles thick, separating them more than anything else ever had.

Something was happening to Chris, and it was suddenly crucial that he understand what she was going through.

"Well," she began tentatively, "I'm not, like, an expert or anything. But, see, what happens is, once a month, the ovaries produce an egg. The egg is what turns into a baby, if it becomes, you know—fertilized, right? So then the uterus, which is where the baby develops, gets all filled out and cushiony, in case there is going be a baby. It needs to be a comfortable place, for the baby to hang out and grow. But if there's no fertilized egg, the uterus just sort of gives up, and then the cushiony lining breaks down and, well, goes away. And that's the flow of blood that comes out."

"Oh." He let this sink in a moment. "Can you feel it . . . happening?"

"Yeah, sort of. Right now there's this kind of dull ache"—she pressed one hand to her abdomen—"down around here. It's not excruciating. But using the tampon, well, that was certainly a whole new . . . uh . . . sensation."

Jack's face flushed. "The box said you can still go swimming," he blurted.

"I know I can go swimming, Jack."

"Oh."

"Were you worried about me not swimming? Like, ever again?"

"No. I just wanted to tell you you could."

"Thanks."

"You're welcome."

A few moments passed, during which Jack tried to distract himself with his fajita, but he was just itching too badly for information. "What about the pads?"

Chris sighed. "What about them?"

"I don't know."

"Well, you can't swim with them, for one thing."

"Who cares about swimming?"

"I thought you did."

"I told you, I just mentioned it because . . ."

"Because we go swimming a lot. Together."

"Yeah, but also because . . . well, I didn't want you to think this was going to change your whole entire life."

"*What?*" Chris's eyes were wide with astonishment. "You think this is gonna change my life?"

"No." He had to bite his lip to keep from adding, "*I hope not.*"

"Well, it's not."

"Of course it's not." Jack shook his head. "One more question?"

"Jack . . ."

"Why today?"

She looked at him funny.

"I mean, why did it show up now, today? Did you do something? Eat something maybe, that could have brought it on?"

"It's not food poisoning, Jack, it's my period. I didn't do anything to 'bring it on.' "

He cleared his throat. "But what about feelings? Couldn't weird feelings, you know, emotions, cause it to happen?"

"It's not a nervous breakdown, either, Jack." She laughed. "But if you keep asking these questions, I might have one of those, too."

Jack frowned. "I'm serious. It's all about hormones,

right? You know, everything we do gets blamed on hormones, so why not this? Maybe, today, for some reason, *today*, your hormones got psyched up or whatever, because you were having some kind of weird feelings about some guy you've never met before and then, the next thing you know . . ."

"Jack . . ."

"Yeah?"

"Shut up and eat."

5

The basketball was in the driveway where they'd left it. Jack scooped it up and carried it into the house.

It was quiet when he opened the front door. But that was nothing new. The house had seemed unnervingly empty, almost dead, since his dad had moved out three weeks earlier. He opened the basement door and without looking tossed the basketball down the dark steps.

"Ouch! Hey!"

"Lukas?" Jack flipped on the light switch and peered down the stairs. His little brother was sitting on the bottom step, rubbing the top of his head.

"What are you doing?"

"Rubbing my head."

"I mean why are you sitting down there in the dark?"

Lukas looked up at Jack over his shoulder. "Thinking."

Jack let out a long rush of breath. He didn't ask what Lukas was thinking about. Or why he was doing it in a darkened basement. He had his own worries.

"Sorry about your head."

"Forget it."

Jack started to close the door.

"Light!"

Jack flicked the switch again, leaving his brother in darkness as he shut the door. He made his way to the kitchen and threw together a sandwich before checking the answering machine. He hit the Play button, then sat down at the kitchen table. The first message was from his father.

"Hi, kids, it's me. Just calling to let you know . . . I'm thinking about you guys, and . . . I miss you."

Jack bit into the sandwich. "So move back," he muttered through a mouthful.

"Uh, the apartment's shaping up nicely," Dad's voice continued nervously. "I'd love it if you'd come by. Maybe Cuff can drive you over." There was an awkward pause on the tape. "Okay. Well. I guess . . . we'll talk soon."

The next call was from the wallpaper guy, apologizing to Jack's mother for the delay with her dining room, but the decorator was slowing him up. Something about coordinating borders and drapery fabric. The last message was for Amy. From Cuff. It was, like, grunt, grunt, call me later, see ya, bye.

Lukas appeared then, and plunked himself down at the kitchen table.

"Mom's going to have an affair with the decorator," he announced.

Jack raised his eyebrows, but kept his voice calm. "Excuse me?"

"It's just a hunch I have."

"Bad hunch, Lukey. Dad may have moved out. And, yeah—Mom's freaked about it. Just like you and me. But she's not going to start dating the decorator." He took another bite of the sandwich. "And anyway, you're grossing me out. You shouldn't even be thinking about this stuff. You should be out building a tree fort or something."

"I'm telling you, Jack. Mom's going to have an affair to get even with Dad, because she thinks *he's* having one, and that that's why he moved out."

Jack frowned. "Did Mom say that?"

"No, I just surprised it."

"I think you mean you *surmised* it."

"Yeah. I figured it out for myself."

"Well, you figured wrong, Luke." Jack swallowed his mouthful and hoped he was right.

Lukas leaned across the table to help himself to the second half of Jack's sandwich. "Know where I was today?"

"Where?"

"Tailing Dad." He chomped off a huge bite of the sandwich. "I can probably talk Mom out of becoming involved with the decorator if I can prove Dad's been faithful."

Jack gave Lukas a sharp look. "How old are you? Forty? Fifty?"

"I'm nine, and you know it. I'm just advanced." Lukas frowned, swallowing. "Especially in the area of family crisis."

Jack couldn't argue with that. They were all becoming well versed in that department. Before Dad moved out, Jack had had a hard time deciding whether it was worse when Mom and Dad were arguing at the top of their lungs or when they went on their cold-shoulder kicks, each pretending the other didn't even exist. He leaned back in his chair and stared at his brother. "So you want to prove Dad's innocent so you can talk Mom out of having a fling with the decorator?"

"Personally," said Lukas, "I think Mom having an affair would go a long way toward clearing the air around here. At the very least, she'll be less frustrated.

I hear extramarital relations can really relax a person."

This was too much! Jack narrowed his eyes at his brother. "What the heck would you know about that?"

"Well, I know that women having affairs get taken out to dinner by their boyfriends, and they get presents and stuff."

"And . . ." Jack prompted.

"And . . ." Lukas shrugged. "I know that dinner and presents would sure make me feel less frustrated and more relaxed."

Jack sighed, relieved at the innocence of the answer. For all Lukas's attempts at sophistication, he really was just a kid.

"You can learn a lot about the way marriages work," explained Lukas, making his exit, "if you keep your ears open around the tennis patio at the club."

After Lukas was gone, Jack didn't get up from his seat at the table. But he just couldn't bring himself to finish his half of the sandwich.

"I'm going to the Summer Cotillion."

No response.

An eerie stillness had fallen over the kitchen. It began the moment Mom had come home, well after seven-thirty, dropped three large sacks of fast food on the table, and gruffly announced, "Dinner."

It had shaken all of them—Jack, Lukas, Amy, even Cuff, who'd eaten over enough times to know that Mrs. Jordan did not consider fast food a suitable dinner. Mrs. Jordan prepared salads and roasts and casseroles and vegetable side dishes, and the rule in the house had always been that no one left the table until they'd consumed at least one item from each of the four food groups.

Jack dragged a french fry through a puddle of ketchup and tried again.

"Mom?"

"Yes, Jack?"

"I'm going to the cotillion. With Chris."

He wasn't sure if she was giving intense thought to his statement, or just mesmerized by watching Cuff as he slowly and systematically flicked sesame seeds off the bun of his burger.

Jack cleared his throat. "I need you to sign the permission form before I can pick up the tickets."

Flick.

"Tickets?"

"To the Summer Cotillion."

"Oh . . . Sure, honey."

Flick.

Lukas let out a little yelp when one of the seeds glanced off his cheek. He gave Cuff a murderous look.

Cuff grinned an apology as Amy reached out to ruffle Lukas's hair and asked casually, "How did the detective work go?"

"Came up empty."

Mom's eyes seemed vacant as she stared at Cuff's burger.

"Hid in the Laundromat across the street from Dad's office for nearly three hours," Lukas continued.

Mom looked away from Cuff's sesame seed excavation long enough to say, "I thought I smelled fabric softener." But she seemed so dazed and distracted that Jack wondered if she even realized what the conversation was about.

"He finally left his building at four," Lukas reported. "Alone. But he was in a hurry."

"Hmm," said Amy, pointedly.

"Precisely." Lukas frowned. "Which is why I went after him the minute he got in his car."

"Did you jump in a cab and shout 'Follow that car!' like they do on TV?" asked Cuff.

"No, I jumped on my bike and pedaled my head off, but I lost sight of him after two blocks." Lukas sighed, pulled a pair of sunglasses out of his shirt pocket, and tossed them on the table. "Perfectly good pair of dark glasses—wasted."

Mom watched Cuff lift the sandwich to his mouth and chomp into it. Sighing, she propped her elbows on the table (more flagrant disregard for house rules) and leaned her chin on her hands. "Did the decorator call?"

Lukas gave Jack a look. Amy gave Cuff the same look.

Jack closed his eyes, trying to determine exactly when his normal, happy family had gone completely nuts. It was just too much to take. His little brother tells them he's resorted to wearing dark glasses and hiding out in the Wash-O-Matic, and his sister just sits there, calmly encouraging him. And Mom, heretofore the steadiest, most grounded individual he had ever known, is oblivious to it all, apparently on some extended sightseeing tour of La-La Land!

Jack decided if he didn't change the subject immediately, he'd go insane on the spot. And the area of most comfort, of course, was Chris.

"Chris needs a dress."

Amy blinked. "Chris? Needs a *dress*?"

"For the cotillion. I was thinking you could help her . . ."

Amy bounced out of her chair so fast she sent Cuff's milk shake skidding across the table.

"Oh, my gosh! I swear, I've been waiting for this chance since the day I met that girl!"

It was a fact not lost on Amy, the Fashion Guru, that the last time Chris had worn a dress was to her mother's funeral, the April that Chris and Jack were in the third grade. He remembered it vividly, from the small, blue collar to the simple white ankle socks she'd worn with it.

His sister began stalking excitedly around the kitchen. "Chris in a dress . . . it'll be the fashion coup of the century! Oh, I *definitely* see her in blue—no, wait—green! Yeah, that'll be *killer* with her hair. I hope she won't freak if I pick out something short—*really* short—because with those legs . . ."

"What legs?"

"*Those* legs!" Amy looked at Jack, her eyes wide with disbelief. "C'mon, little brother. Don't even tell me you never noticed your best friend's gams before."

"Chris does have lovely legs," Mrs. Jordan confirmed, with a halfhearted nod.

Jack was trying to picture Chris's legs. Only today he'd noticed her hair, and her eyes, as if he'd never seen them before . . . quite by accident, of course, but he had noticed. He made a mental note to pay more attention to her legs. Wasn't she always joking about her knees being knobby?

Amy's eyes were practically glowing. "She's going to look beautiful."

"Beautiful," murmured Mom.

"Beautiful," echoed Lukas.

"Not too beautiful."

Jack heard the words, but he wasn't sure at first if

he was the one who had spoken them. Judging by the curious looks he was getting from his family, he must have been. *Not too beautiful.* It sounded like a warning. Or a plea.

Whatever it was, it seemed to call for an explanation. He cleared his throat.

"I mean . . . you know . . . don't go overboard or anything. It's just the cotillion. And I know Chris. She won't be comfortable if you make her too beautiful."

Amy squinted at him, then said, "Shut up, Jack."

Cuff laughed and stuffed the remainder of his burger into his mouth.

Lukas picked up his sunglasses and put them on. "I wonder if there's any way we could break into Dad's new place and tap the phone."

Mom, glumly sipping the remains of her milk shake, didn't seem to hear him.

Jack rolled his eyes, and suddenly the cheeseburger he'd eaten felt like lead in his stomach. All he wanted to do was escape the surreal atmosphere of his kitchen table. He knew there was only one thing that would take his mind off short dresses, and unfaithful fathers.

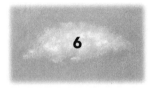

6

Coincidentally—or perhaps not—Jack had discovered his artistic talent right around the time that he'd discovered Chris. He had fallen in love with drawing in the first grade, which was when Chris had fallen in love with sports.

Jack closed his bedroom door behind him, picked up his sketchbook from his desk, and planted himself on the bed. Before he opened the sketchbook, he glanced around the room, taking comfort in the fact that he was surrounded by his artwork. Some of it was framed, but the majority had just been torn from the pad and tacked up on the walls.

Near the foot of his bed was one of the best pen-and-ink sketches Jack had ever made, circa sixth grade. It was a waist-up rendering of Chris during a tennis match, preparing to execute her infamous overhead smash. From the dramatic extension of her forearm to the smudgy spin of the ball in flight, the drawing was as perfect as he could get.

Chris had been very proud of him for that drawing. She'd said it was so lifelike that when she looked at it she kept waiting to hear the ball hit her racquet.

Jack opened the book on his lap, his most current, and began to thumb through it. He paused at one he'd done months ago, of a tennis racquet—Chris's racquet. She'd helped him choose the colors, insisting he replicate *exactly* the purple and yellow of its splashy lettering. The real challenge had been in getting the grip right, shading it just so to indicate how worn and smooth and contoured it was. There was something so loved, so comfortable about the condition of that grip, and somehow, he'd captured it.

Several of the sketches were of Chris herself, smiling, or scowling in concentration as she prepared to shoot a basket; there was even one of her asleep on her sofa. Odd, he decided suddenly, that these were all in black and white.

On an impulse, he reached for his colored pencils. His fingers lingered over the box a moment before he selected sepia. He leaned over one of his favorite sketches—her face in profile—and began to add color to the light gray iris. He added a touch—just a touch—of gold, which he softened gently with the side of his thumb. Black for the pupil and white, of course, to suggest reflected light.

A strange rush of anticipation filled him as he replaced the white pencil and reached for the orange. He frowned at it, knowing that, on its own, it was all wrong for her hair, would make her look like Raggedy Ann. He'd blend the gold over it, perhaps some bronze. He worked intensely, first with one pencil and then with another.

Then he moved on to her skin, which was a hue that fell somewhere between peach and tawny, depending upon the season of the year. Of course, there was also that troublesome bloom of pink he'd seen today, when Sam had come to retrieve the tennis ball. Jack added it, reluctantly but conscientiously, circling, smudging, sweeping his rose pencil until it yielded the warm, petal-soft color he remembered.

He added a hint of color to her eyebrows, then finished with her lips, which needed delicate, careful work.

When he was through, Jack leaned back against the headboard and examined what he'd done. He was amazed. Not by his drawing, exactly. But by her. *She* amazed him.

Not too beautiful, he'd told his sister.

Yeah, right.

He studied the drawing for a long moment, wishing he knew why the stupid thing was having such a strong effect on him. He wondered absently if Lukas was right, if their father was seeing another woman— and if he was, was she beautiful? Odds were, she was stunning.

Shoving the thought aside, he flipped through the sketchbook pages again, slowly this time, just to see if he'd ever bothered to do a drawing that included his best friend's legs.

Unfortunately, he hadn't.

Yet.

7

He was hanging out with Chris in the small den of her apartment.

It wasn't just *her* apartment, of course, but sometimes it felt that way, since lately her father was spending more and more time with Soxie. Usually Jack found the Moffetts' cozy little apartment relaxing. Living above Hot Rollers meant the apartment always smelled faintly of expensive hair products. The exposed eaves and intricate millwork appealed to the artist in him. He liked the old-fashioned casement windows, which overlooked the cobblestones and gaslights of Eastport's Main Street, with its elegant eateries and pricey shops. The noises of the busy street had a pleasant way of drifting in through the windows. It was nothing at all like Jack's neighborhood, where long, winding driveways and strategically placed Japanese maples ensured seclusion and silence. Except, of course, when there was a lot of screaming and shouting going on inside the house.

Today, though, Jack was too busy pacing to relax.

"Jack," said Chris, not looking up from the sports page, "will you please stop pacing?"

"I'm not pacing."

She kept reading. "Yes, you are."

Jack forced himself to a standstill, planting himself beside Chris's desk and reading over her shoulder.

"Worse than pacing, Jack."

"Sorry."

Chris put down the paper and turned to face him. "Listen, if anybody should be pacing, it's me. You're a member of the stupid club. I'm only going swimming with you because"—she cocked an eyebrow at him—"tell me again why I'm going. Chaperone? Or bodyguard, maybe?"

"Emily said to bring you along. I guess she figured the more the merrier."

"How charitable of her."

"It's not like that."

Chris gave him a look, then stood up and headed for her room. Jack followed, watching as she rooted through a dresser drawer.

"I've got to tell you, Jack. I think it's a tad arrogant of little Miss Baskin to invite you to your own country club."

Jack sighed. "I told you, she didn't invite me. She just called and asked if I was going to be at the pool today."

Chris turned to face him. "Why? I mean, since when would she care?"

The remark did not sting, because Jack had been wondering the same thing himself.

"I don't know," he admitted. "She just said that she hoped I would be there, since everybody . . ."

"Everybody," muttered Chris disdainfully.

". . . since everybody was going to be there, and it would be a lot of fun. And then she said to bring you."

"Surprised she even remembered my name."

Emily Baskin, a year younger than Jack, but a lifetime more popular, occasionally deigned to say hello to him at the club, but she'd never—*never*—called him on the phone before. Until last Wednesday, the day after Jack and Chris had played tennis. He'd answered the phone, hoping it wouldn't be the decorator, whose most recent phone messages to Mom had managed to make wallpaper paste sound sexy.

"Hello?"

"Jack? Hi."

She hadn't identified herself, and in spite of his shock, it did occur to Jack that it was pretty egotistical of her to just assume he'd recognize her voice. He *did* recognize her voice, but that wasn't the point.

"Emily. Hi."

"Hey, so, how come you haven't been around the club much?"

"Uh . . ."

"You're, like, never at the pool."

He'd almost felt as if he should apologize. Before he could, though, she'd made him promise he'd be there on Saturday, because "everybody" would be there and it was supposed to be a totally nice day, and they'd totally have fun, and, hey, maybe if his friend Chris wasn't busy, she could come, too.

"Chris?"

There was a pause, and he thought he heard something muffling the mouthpiece at her end of the line. Could lip gloss interfere with telephone reception? he wondered.

But the muffling subsided and she answered, "Yeah. Chris."

He'd agreed to be there around eleven, and Emily had giggled a good-bye. Heck, he'd felt a little like giggling himself.

He'd never been part of that "everybody" crowd, although he wanted to be. Sure, he knew them all, and they knew him. He wore the right clothes, and got dropped off at school and the club in the right kinds of cars, and he definitely lived in the right neighborhood. But for some reason, he'd always seemed stuck on the outskirts of that glittering circle.

Chris knew he wanted in. Chris thought it was ridiculous and she never let him forget it.

"Wanting to be popular isn't illegal," he'd tell her whenever she bugged him about it.

"No," she'd say sweetly. "Just insane."

So Jack figured Chris agreeing to join him today had less to do with her support of his cause than it did with the fact that Sam the Tennis God (whom, to the best of his knowledge, she still hadn't had the courage to call) might be in the vicinity.

He shrugged. "Lighten up. It'll be fun."

"Fun, huh?" Chris tugged something out of the drawer. "Then why are you pacing?"

"Why aren't you?" he tossed back playfully. "Sam's gonna be there."

He noticed a slight hesitation. But her recovery was quick, and she flipped her bangs out of her eyes.

"Yeah? So?"

Jack was about to reply, but then he noticed something that stopped him cold. "What's that?"

"What?"

"That!" He motioned to the two scraps of fabric she was holding.

"It's my bathing suit."

Jack blinked. "Where's the rest of it?"

"Top," she said, holding up the skimpy bra-like portion. "And bottom." She dangled the even skimpier lower half from her thumb. "What else is there?"

"You usually wear a one-piece."

"I know." She shrugged. "Amy talked me into buying this one."

"Oh."

"Is there a problem?"

"No."

"Good. Now"—she made a little shooing gesture with her hand—"get out so I can change."

Jack obeyed; he had the den to himself for exactly two seconds before he heard the sound of the door being unlocked at the bottom of the stairs.

"Chris?" her dad called as he pulled the door shut behind him.

"She's getting changed," Jack replied over the sound of Mr. Moffett's heavy footsteps on the stairs. In seconds, he was standing in the kitchen, and Jack had to struggle to hide his surprise. It was evident, from his tousled hair and the rumpled appearance of his clothing, that the guy had not come home last night.

Which meant, of course, that Chris had been alone.

All alone. All night.

Jack frowned. Mr. Moffett must have understood, because he responded with a sheepish look.

"I know, I know . . ." He lifted his hands as if Jack were holding him at gunpoint. "But it's not as bad as it looks, really." He jerked his thumb over his shoulder, indicating the apartment next door. "I knew Mrs. Donohue would be home . . ."

Jack couldn't imagine the ninety-three-year-old Mrs. Donohue being much help in an emergency.

". . . so I asked her to keep an ear tuned in case Chris needed her."

Jack wondered if that ear would be the one with or without the hearing aid.

Of course, respect for his elders prevented him from voicing his thoughts out loud. Respect for elders, *and* the fact that Mr. Moffett was six-four and had one of those weight lifter's physiques which, even as he spoke, rippled at Jack from beneath the wrinkled dress shirt.

"So what's new, kid? How're the folks?"

"Fine."

Mr. Moffett poured himself a glass of juice. The movement crunched up his right biceps until it was roughly the size of a cantaloupe.

"What are you and Chris up to today?"

"We're going to the club. Meeting some friends."

"Nice day for it." He lifted the glass to his lips and took a long swallow.

Chris opened her bedroom door just then, and scowled when she saw her father.

"Hey, honey."

Chris murmured a curt hello, shooting her friend a let's-get-out-of-here look, which Jack hardly noticed.

He was too relieved by the fact that, over that skimpy excuse for a swimsuit she'd shown him, Chris was wearing a very predictable pair of running shorts and her favorite beat-up T-shirt, the one with the statement I STINK, THEREFORE I RAN emblazoned across the back.

Mr. Moffett gave her a weak smile. "You're wearing that to the club?"

"Yes." Chris finally eyed him directly. "Or maybe you think I should wear the same clothes I wore last night?"

Mr. Moffett surprised Jack by looking away.

Then Chris snatched up her backpack, from which the handle of her racquet protruded. "Let's go already."

8

They found Emily Baskin and her crowd in what Jack had always regarded as the prime section of the pool area, a portion of the patio that boasted not only full sun all day but also easy access to the diving boards and the canteen for cold soda and snacks. It also featured plenty of breathing room from the crowd of mommies and little kids at the shallow end of the pool.

Chris dropped her stuff onto a chaise longue. Jack hadn't brought anything, since everything he needed was stored neatly in the locker he shared with his father.

"I've got to go change and grab us some towels," he said softly to Chris.

A flicker of panic crossed her face, and Jack felt instantly guilty for leaving her alone. First her father, now him, he thought. Unfortunately, here on the patio, Chris did not have old Mrs. Donohue to protect her.

"I'll only be a second," he promised in a whisper, then nodded toward a girl in a green bikini. "Talk to Kara. You guys know each other. Sort of."

Chris nodded glumly as Jack turned on his heel and took off across the patio.

The dressing area of the men's locker room was large enough to house a family of eight, and, were it not for the smell of deodorant and the presence of hundreds of metal lockers, it could easily have been mistaken for the library of some old English manor house, with its mossy green carpet and wood-paneled walls hung with aristocratic scenes of golfing and fox hunting.

Jack jerked open his dad's locker. His bathing suit was looped over a hook toward the front. He took it and changed quickly, stuffing his clothes into the locker and accidentally knocking a pair of his father's tennis shorts to the floor.

A slip of paper was poking out from the pocket of the shorts. Before he could stop himself, Jack was removing it. I'm as bad as Lukey, he thought. As soon as

Jack read what was written on the paper, he wished he hadn't.

Melissa, 555-3248.

Lukas was right. Amy was right.

Their father was seeing someone. Someone, evidently, named Melissa.

"Jordan?"

Jack crumpled the note and, having nowhere better to put it, returned it to the pocket of the shorts. Then he turned to see Kyle Baskin, Emily's older brother and Chris's first-grade crush, along with Davis Everett, standing behind him.

"Jordan. What's up?"

Jack took two of the snowy white club towels from the neat pile arranged on a table. He slung them over his shoulder and gave Kyle what he hoped was a careless grin. "Hey. How's it going?"

"Glad you could make it." Kyle made the statement with a cocky grin, as if he were welcoming Jack to a private party at his house. It made Jack remember Chris's comment about Emily having the nerve to invite Jack to his own club . . .

Jack wasn't sure how to reply, so he didn't, just fell into step with the two as they headed out of the locker room. He forced his worry about Melissa to the back of his mind and resolved not to think about it for the rest of the afternoon. He wasn't about to let his father's sleazy behavior ruin this day for him.

Kyle and his buddy took to the patio like a pair of popular actors taking the stage. What was strange to Jack was that the illusion was created not so much by the way Kyle and his sidekick were acting as by the way the rest of the crowd was *re*acting.

The younger girls turned to stare with dreamy eyes; the older ones, lifeguards included, looked at them with a mixture of fondness and amusement. The mommies in the kiddie section were smiling, too. Who knew what they were thinking?

Jack couldn't help but wonder if that was how he, in the past, had reacted to Kyle and the rest. He knew he did his best to try to ignore them from his lonely chaise longue. But he was watching. And they knew it.

Suddenly, Kyle stopped walking. He seemed captivated by something he saw on the opposite side of the pool.

Jack followed Kyle's gaze to see what had caused him to stop dead in his tracks. Then Jack saw the reason. She waved. He waved back.

After all, Chris was his best friend.

Jack turned to Kyle and saw he was grinning again. But this grin didn't look as cocky as it did . . . *silly*. Jack had a sudden urge to wipe the stupid thing right off Baskin's face.

He looked across the pool again, to where Chris was squirting some suntan lotion into her palm. Why was he getting the distinct feeling that she was in danger?

"Your buddy Chris . . ." Kyle began, then cleared his throat. "She still into tennis?"

"Yeah, she's still—"

"How 'bout soccer. She still play soccer?"

"Sometimes." Jack stuffed his hands into the pockets of his swim trunks. "Why?"

Kyle gave a casual shrug. "She just looks . . . I don't know, *different*."

"What do you mean, 'different'?" Jack asked stiffly.

"I don't know. She looks like maybe she doesn't play all that much soccer anymore."

Jack wondered if Kyle realized how stupid that sounded. How does someone look like they don't play soccer?

At that moment, Chris leaned over to smear the lotion on her shins. As if that were the cue, Kyle and Davis started moving again; Jack found himself a step behind. When they arrived at the place where the girls were seated, Kyle walked directly to Chris.

Jack could tell she was surprised, but she didn't faint, or fall off her chaise longue or anything. She even managed a grin.

Kyle's grin was designed to throw heat; one look at Chris's reddening cheeks told Jack it was working. And then, in his mind, Jack heard the echo of a conversation from the distant past. "Only Kyle Baskin can . . ."

In the present, Kyle was saying, "Hi . . . Christy."

In that second, Jack had a sudden, ridiculous vision of Kyle asking Chris to marry him then and there.

But Kyle simply reached out nonchalantly to a spot of lotion on Chris's shoulder and used his thumb to smooth it into her skin. He was working his magic, taking his time. It seemed like two hundred years went by before he finally said, "I was thinking we could play tennis later."

What the heck was *this*? Was *every* good-looking guy in Eastport suddenly going to seek out Chris Moffett and invite her to play tennis?

Then Kyle was telling Chris—make that *Christy*—that he already had a court reserved for this afternoon.

"Well . . . um . . ." She turned to Jack, as if he had first dibs on her afternoon schedule. Jack took some comfort in the fact that it visibly displeased Baskin. "Mind if I play tennis with Kyle later?" she asked.

Jack shrugged. "No. Go ahead."

His only consolation was that Chris would undoubtedly wipe up the court with Kyle Baskin.

Things were looking up.

More specifically, *Emily* was looking up. Up and

into Jack's eyes. He'd just removed his blue polo shirt, and as he tossed it onto the last free chaise longue, he noticed that Emily's eyes were making a slow trek upward, from his stomach to his chest, with a quick shift to each shoulder. She was darn bold for a girl who'd only just finished seventh grade.

When her gaze finally reached his, he was pleased to note that there was a quiver of surprise in it.

"What?" he asked; he knew "what," he just wanted to hear her say it.

"You're kinda built. Like, seriously."

Jack gave her a smile that was both proud and embarrassed. She was right, and he knew he had Chris to thank for it. A year ago she'd put him on a weight-training regimen, and it had paid off. Jack's body was slowly becoming a scaled-down version of Mr. Moffett's, although, if Emily's reaction was any indication, maybe not as slowly as he'd thought.

He took his place on the chaise longue next to Emily's, listening to the various threads of conversation around him. Davis was bragging about his brother's new car; Molly was oohing over Kara's ankle bracelet. Kyle was leaning close to Chris, murmuring something. He wished he could think of something dazzling to say to Emily, but she'd turned her attention to the magazine in her lap.

Jack took the opportunity to study her in profile,

and after a minute or so he reluctantly admitted to himself that the view was not perfect. Her nose had something of a pinched quality about it, and her chin was a little too pointy. She didn't score overly well in the cheekbone department either.

This bothered Jack. Of all people, Emily Baskin was *supposed* to be perfect. At least, Jack had spent the better part of his childhood thinking she was. She was one of the Beautiful People—and wasn't that expression meant to apply literally?

He looked closer; there was no denying she was attractive. Extremely. Pretty mouth, an almost exotic slant to her eyes, a cute figure. But while these individual components, combined, did create head-turning results, they did not add up to perfection.

The perfection, Jack was beginning to understand, came in the form of enhancements, such as the costly swimsuit, the professional manicure, and the very appealing backdrop of the E.C.C.

And then there was that other thing, that priceless, all-important ingredient which somehow could bump even a mediocre-looking person to the next echelon.

That ingredient was attitude.

And, without question, Emily Baskin had it—enough of it, in fact, to smooth the point of her chin, improve the shape of her nose. Emily Baskin even had enough attitude to create the illusion of cheekbones.

Attitude, Jack suddenly understood, was more effective than plastic surgery.

His artistic perception was fired up now, and he decided to make a thoroughly aesthetic study of the people surrounding him. As an artist, objectively.

Davis had a strong jaw but a short neck, and his eyebrows were incompatible—with each other, as well as with the rest of his face.

Molly's teeth were straight but too big; her lips were plump in the wrong places.

Kyle's eyes were a bit wide-set, and he was bow-legged.

Kara was basically cute, once you got past that ski jump of a nose.

Merely for comparison's sake, Jack considered his own looks.

He knew his pale eyes, the silvery green of willow leaves, were his best feature. Jack, unlike Emily, had cheekbones—not chiseled necessarily, but well defined. He'd always been told he looked a lot like his father, who apparently made quite a romantic impression on the Melissas of the world. He had his mother's hair—a rich chestnut brown. And, as Emily had so brazenly pointed out, he was becoming rather built.

On the downside, he'd always felt his small, round nose would be better suited to a teddy bear than an actual human being, and one of his eyeteeth slightly overlapped the tooth beside it.

Jack processed this information with a mixture of disappointment and delight. The startling truth was that here, among the Beautiful People, Jack Jordan was as good-looking as anyone . . . if you didn't count Chris, who, with her delicate features and tumbling cherry-gold hair, by anybody's standards had somehow overnight become a knockout—and this accomplished with no attitude whatsoever.

It was her attitude-free good looks—long hidden under baggy sweatshirts and overshadowed by her tomboy sense of style—that had Kyle Baskin reeling now.

Chris, in minutes, had managed to do what Jack himself had silently been striving for since the day he was old enough to sign for lunch at the snack bar on his parents' account. Just by showing up, she'd broken through the force field that had kept him on the outside of that wonderful, magical circle.

Okay . . . so, *how*?

Maybe, Jack decided, watching as Chris stood and walked confidently toward the pool—maybe what Chris had was something beyond attitude, something attitude could only aspire to be when it grew up.

She moved toward the three-meter board, and it occurred to Jack, with a mixture of pride and envy, that she looked more like a member than the members did. She didn't care that the plastic chair slats had left red imprints on the backs of her thighs, she didn't mind that her ponytail had gone askew, and she certainly didn't act as if she was trying to get everyone's attention while maintaining the appearance of not trying to get everyone's attention. She didn't care about everyone's attention, but she had it nonetheless.

Chris positioned herself three paces from the end of the board. She made an elegant approach, circling her arms through her launch, then vaulted herself into the crystalline water of the Eastport Country Club swimming pool. Jack couldn't help but view it symbolically. It was a baptism—a baptism in the form of a flawless front flip in pike position.

Molly and Kara indicated their approval, oohing in harmony. Emily looked up briefly, acknowledging the dive by wrinkling her nose when the splash speckled the pages of her magazine.

Chris broke through the surface smiling, her long ponytail swinging off silvery droplets of water, her gracefully rounded shoulders glistening in the sun.

That was *his* best friend, gliding now toward the deep-end ladder.

When Chris emerged from the pool, Kyle plucked her towel from the chaise longue and met her halfway. Like that meant something? Jack had to stop himself from huffing out a chuckle. Sure, bring her a towel, he scoffed silently. When she lets you borrow her hockey skates, or sends *you* to the store for feminine-hygiene products, *then* we'll talk!

Feeling happy and smug, he leaned back in his chair and relaxed. He took a long breath of the sunscreen-scented air. The sun warmed his face and chest, the water lapped lazily at the tiled edges of the enormous pool, and Emily Baskin was beside him.

Jack Jordan's world was, at last, setting itself to rights. The circumference of that glittering circle was finally expanding to include him.

And what was even better was that he could bring his best friend along for the ride.

A noxious thought wafted by like the scent of chlorine, but Jack dismissed it firmly. It was Chris who'd be coming along for the ride with him. Not the other way around.

9

By lunchtime, Jack was feeling wildly confident.

After Kyle had "accidentally" dropped his sister's magazine into the deep end, Emily had been thoroughly attentive to Jack—all over him, in fact, taking great pains to keep him as far away from Chris as she could. Apparently, she was the possessive type, because each time he'd attempted to talk to Chris, Emily had dragged him away, or cut him off, once by throwing her arms around his neck and shrieking for him to protect her from a yellow jacket.

Chris had rolled her eyes and whopped the insect with her tennis shoe.

At one o'clock, Kyle announced it was time for a

trip to the grill room. That meant shirts and sneakers and combed hair.

It also meant, Jack discovered when they reached the restaurant, separate tables. A large round one for himself, Emily, Davis, Kara, and Molly, and a table for two, in the corner, for Kyle and Chris. The tables were adjacent, but very definitely separate.

As the hostess led them to their seats, he checked Chris's expression; she didn't seem to mind—after all, she'd been waiting for this moment since the first grade. Jack slid into his chair, wishing he'd thought of getting a table alone with Emily.

Too late now.

Next time.

When the hostess was gone, Kyle turned and reminded Davis that today lunch was on the Fiedlers.

"Wow," said Jack. "Pretty nice of Dr. Fiedler to buy us lunch."

Emily giggled. "It would be," she said, "if he knew about it."

Jack looked at her, confused.

"We never sign our own names when we eat in here," said Kara. Jack thought he heard a note of reluctance in her voice.

"Kyle figured out we could just charge it to someone else's account," Emily whispered, her voice full of reverence for her brother's criminal antics. "It's not like anyone ever checks the signatures." She giggled again. "It's a total goof."

Jack blinked, trampling the urge to get up and walk out of the restaurant. What had Dr. Fiedler ever done to them, he wondered, that the guy should have to spring for seven cheeseburgers, and who knew how many sodas and side orders? But since the girls were clearly impressed with Kyle's conniving, Jack didn't voice an opinion.

Beside him, Molly was fumbling in her purse for an emery board. So far, the hunt had produced a lipstick, two barrettes, and four eyeliner pencils, which rolled across the tablecloth toward Jack. Inspiration struck.

"Check this out," he said. He unfolded his white linen napkin and uncapped a black kohl eyeliner.

Molly started to protest but stopped short when she saw what he did next.

The point of the makeup pencil made a clean line on his napkin. Then another. In seconds, Jack had sketched the oval beginnings of a face.

Emily gasped, then giggled.

Davis grinned, probably more at Jack's brazen willingness to deface club property than at his artistry. Kara cooed her appreciation as soon as she recognized that the face Jack was drawing was hers. She was sitting directly across from Jack, and the light from the tall windows of the grill room was just right.

Jack could feel Chris's disapproval radiating from the next table, but he kept sketching. He switched to a brown waterproof liner for the hair, which he achieved with long, sweeping strokes. After that, he used Molly's frosted lip liner to add Kara's mouth, then filled it in with the lipstick.

The sketch was a masterpiece. The napkin was ruined. Kara was delighted.

"I didn't know you could, like, draw," Emily said.

Molly was already fishing in her bag for more supplies. "Do one for me," she pleaded, handing him a compact of powder blush, some grayish purple powdered eye shadow, and a fresh napkin.

In minutes, he'd sketched a remarkable rendering of Molly. The powder gave it an impressionistic effect.

Jack's art show, as it turned out, saved Dr. Fiedler a pretty penny; when the waiter arrived to take their order and spotted the graffiti, he immediately dismissed them from the dining room.

Kyle and Chris, at their separate table with its unsullied linens, were allowed to stay.

That only bothered Jack for a moment.

Because Emily Baskin was holding his hand.

Emily held his hand all the way back to the pool area but said nothing. Sneaking a glance in her direction, Jack saw that she seemed deep in thought over something and decided to keep his mouth shut. When they reached their chaise longues, Emily turned to him with a pout.

"Why didn't you draw me?"

Jack thought fast. "I was saving the best for last," he told her, hoping it didn't sound as corny to her as it did to him. Clearly, it didn't. Her pout turned into a dazzling smile.

"Well, then, I've got two words for you," she bubbled.

"What are they?"

"Co. Tillion."

Jack blinked. "What about it?"

"I want you to take me." She sighed, dramatically. "That's why it's called a *co*-tillion. Because you go *with* someone."

What could she possibly think *tillion* meant? he wondered. "I'd love to take you," he said, trying not to dwell on her definition, or the fact that he'd already roped Chris into going with him.

"Great. So will you promise me something?"

"What?"

"Will you bring, like, crayons, or markers, or whatever you usually draw with?"

"Pencils?"

Emily nodded; her expensive haircut showed itself off. "How come?"

"Duh. So you can draw pictures of *me*." She hesitated, as something occurred to her. "You can draw pictures of *everybody*," she gushed, then leaned in closer to him, with a conspiratorial smile. "We'll *so* be the center of attention!"

"Oh." Jack felt a pang of worry. It sounded like a pretty self-serving stunt. And, anyway, how many perfectly good table linens could he bring himself to ruin? "Well . . ."

Emily gave him another pout: her secret weapon. It worked.

"Markers. Okay. Pencils. Sure. And a sketch pad." At least he wouldn't have to defile any more napkins.

Satisfied, Emily lowered herself to her chair and turned her full attention to the sun.

Pleats.

She was wearing *pleats*!

A lampshade's worth of them, circling her hips, fluttering in the late-afternoon breeze.

Chris Moffett in a tennis skirt. A white, pleated tennis skirt with a sky blue stripe around the bottom that complemented the scallop-edged, sky blue tank top she wore over it.

It was an out-and-out *outfit*!

Jack almost choked when he saw her on the court. She was wrapping a sky blue scrunchie into her hair, holding her racquet between her knees, and smiling at Kyle, who was smiling at her.

What happened to I STINK, THEREFORE I RAN? Jack wondered.

Emily came up beside him now, in a sleeveless cotton dress with a flouncy bottom and a polo collar. Her tennis sneakers probably cost as much as Davis's brother's new car.

She, like Jack, was frowning at Chris's outfit, although Jack suspected her reasons were different from his own.

"No courts," Emily huffed.

"What about theirs?" He motioned toward Chris and Kyle.

"They're *on* it," she snapped.

"I know. Maybe they'll want to play doubles."

Emily shook her head. "Kyle said—" She stopped abruptly.

"Kyle said what?"

"Nothing." She shrugged. "I just don't think they'll want to."

Jack decided to ask anyway. He opened the gate and stepped onto the court.

"How about some mixed doubles?" he called. The tone of his voice fell somewhere between that of a friendly invitation and that of a declaration of war.

"No, thanks," said Kyle.

At the same time, Chris was saying, "Yeah, sure."

"Great." Jack moved toward Chris, smiling. "Nice outfit," he said under his breath. "Beat up some cheerleader for it?"

Chris smiled back, narrowing her eyes. "What about Emily's?" she hissed. "If it were any shorter, Jack, it'd be a headband."

"Jealous?"

"Please!"

He squinted at her. "Are you wearing makeup?"

She glanced away. His point.

"Since when do you wear makeup?" he demanded in a harsh whisper.

"Since ten minutes ago in the locker room. Molly wanted to experiment."

"So now you're a lab rat?"

"And now *you're* the cosmetics police?" She gave him a hard look. "Makeup, Jack. It's not just for cloth napkins anymore."

"Funny."

They were interrupted by a tennis ball colliding with Jack's hip. Both of them whirled to see Kyle, attempting to look apologetic.

He shrugged. "Sorry."

Emily was admiring her tan against the white of her tennis socks. "So are we gonna, like, play, or what?"

"Yeah," said Jack. "Let's play."

10

After half an hour, Jack realized that Emily was good at two things: keeping score. And keeping her fingernails out of danger, by avoiding the ball at all costs.

"Love–forty," she announced when Jack pounded the ball in Chris's direction.

"That was in," Jack barked.

Emily examined her manicure. "Looked out to me."

Across the court, Chris smiled.

It was the smile that inspired Jack's next three unreturnable serves—two for Chris, one for Kyle.

"Deuce!"

Kyle pulled himself together to score his first and

only point; it was a meteorlike shot that sent Jack toward the fence to retrieve the ball.

That was when he noticed Sam. He was sitting in the same spot where Chris had been sitting the day Sam had pulled that ultra-smooth, phone-number-on-the-tennis-ball move.

He was watching intently, but something told Jack it was not out of love for the game.

He didn't look angry exactly. More like crushed.

In a show of brilliant strategy, Jack lifted his racquet in acknowledgment. "Hi, Sam!"

Chris turned in Sam's direction, and Jack could see the embarrassment flicker across her face. She hadn't called *him* to play tennis, but here she was, teamed up with Kyle Baskin, decked out in an ensemble that was the epitome of cute. She managed a wave, just as Kyle, employing some strategy of his own, appeared at her side to drape his arm around her waist.

Sam waved back. Poor guy, Jack thought with a smile. Chris seemed to read his mind. She shot Jack a ninety-five-mile-an-hour look, which Jack returned. Then Kyle was at the net again, and Chris moved into position to receive.

Jack slammed her his best serve of the day.

She punished him with an effortless forehand that sent the ball screaming back at him, inches shy of Emily's ear.

Jack scuffed sideways and connected with his backhand.

But Chris knew Jack's backhand as well as she knew her own heartbeat; predicting the ball's short flight, she rushed the net and popped back a slick volley that landed hard at Emily's feet.

Emily jumped backward, squealing and covering her face with her racquet.

"That's game," Kyle announced smugly, either unaware or unconcerned that he'd had nothing whatsoever to do with it. He was still standing in the same spot he'd been in since Jack had served.

Jack gave Emily an encouraging nod. "We'll win the next one."

"No, thanks," she said flatly. "I'm done."

"What about the rest of the match?" he asked, a bit desperately.

Emily shrugged. "I'm not in the mood."

Since when did sports protocol depend on a mood? Jack wondered.

In the grand tennis tradition, their opponents were approaching the net to shake hands. Chris reached over it to fold her fingers around Jack's; for a moment, he was afraid she might try to break his knuckles. He was surprised to feel her hand tremble.

Her eyes darted quickly toward Sam, then back to

meet Jack's. "Real nice, Jack," she muttered. "Real nice."

Instantly, he felt like a jerk. He opened his mouth to apologize, but she was already heading off the court, with Emily practically skipping along beside her, shamelessly singing her brother's praises. Kyle followed at a calculated distance; Jack passed him without a word.

When they reached the gate, Sam was holding it open. "Hi."

Chris smiled awkwardly. "Hi."

"Good game."

"Thanks."

Emily flashed Sam a brilliant grin, which he didn't seem to notice. Jack noted vaguely that maybe Emily's staring at Sam should bother him, but he was too hypnotized by the current of tension flowing between Chris and Sam.

"I thought you and I were going to . . . I mean, I was hoping you'd call."

"I was going to," Chris answered quickly. "But I've been . . . well . . . I haven't had a chance . . ."

"I guess not." Sam glanced at Kyle, who was sidling up to Chris and looking very possessive.

For a long moment, Sam and Kyle just looked at each other. Then Kyle broke the silence with a chuckle.

"Better luck next time," he said. Actually, he sort of snickered it. Even cockier than usual.

Sam's eyes flashed, and for a second Jack expected to see Kyle going headfirst through the fence. It was anybody's guess, though, whether it would be Sam or Chris who would do it to him. Not that it would matter to Jack; he'd just like to see it happen.

Then Charlie, the tennis pro, was there, demanding a moment of Kyle's time—something about stolen grip tape. Emily tore her eyes away from Sam, shrugged Jack a good-bye, and loyally followed her brother and Charlie toward the pro shop.

Standing there with Chris and Sam, Jack felt both conspicuous and invisible.

"So, do you really want to get together for a game?" Sam asked, his voice serious. "Or are you just being . . . you know . . . nice?"

"I really want to," Chris assured him. "I do."

Sam nodded in the direction of the pro shop. "What about . . . ?"

"Kyle?"

"Yeah. Is he, like . . . are you two . . . ?"

"No. It's not like that. He's . . . just . . . you know . . . a friend."

Just . . . you know . . . a friend . . . The words burned in Jack's ears. He knew she was referring to Kyle, but still . . .

Sam relaxed a little. "Oh. Okay, so . . . how about tomorrow? Want to play tomorrow?"

Jack held his breath. But this time Chris didn't consult him.

She accepted with a smile. A smile full of sincerity and tinted with rose-colored lip gloss.

When Jack got home, he found his father sitting on the front porch.

"Hi, Dad."

"Hi."

"What are you doin' out here?"

"I came by to pick up some things. But Lukas won't let me in. Not unless I'm staying."

There was a catch in his father's voice that made Jack almost feel sorry for him. Then he remembered Melissa and felt sick.

Jack sat down on the step. "He's having a hard time with this," he said. *We all are.* His dad sighed, then motioned to the tennis racquet in Jack's hand.

"Good game?"

"Not really."

"Who'd you play?"

"Kyle Baskin."

Mr. Jordan's eyebrows rose slightly. He was obviously surprised, but, Jack could tell, he was trying not to show it. "Oh."

They sat quietly for a moment. Then Jack announced, "I'm going to the cotillion."

"I know. With Chris." His father smiled. "Mom told me."

This momentarily stunned Jack. *Mom* told him? When? And in what context had she told him? Had they managed somehow to engage in a civil conversation recently? Or did the sentence "Jack's going to the dance with Chris" come shrieking on the heels of "You lying, two-timing dirtbag!"

Jack winced at a sudden pain near his temples; the word *two-timing* struck a chord.

"I was going with Chris," he said glumly. "But now I'm taking Emily."

There went his dad's brows again. "Baskin?" This time his shock went unmasked.

"Yeah. *She* asked *me*. I'm going to bring my pencils and junk, and draw pictures of everybody. According to Emily, we'll be a big hit."

His father took a moment to digest the information. "Is Chris glad to be off the hook?"

"I'll let you know as soon as I tell her."

"Ahhhh." Mr. Jordan leaned forward, resting his elbows on his knees, and nodded sympathetically. "Two dates."

Jack bristled at the understanding tone in his father's voice. Clearly, the guy could relate. He half expected his old man to throw an arm around him, chuckle proudly, and call Jack a "chip off the old block."

But, to Jack's relief, his father said nothing of the kind, just sat there beside his son and allowed an awkward silence to pass.

After a while, his dad stood up and said he had to go. "I'll come back another time," he said. "I don't want to get Lukas more upset than he is. Do me a favor, Jack—go inside and talk to him. Try to help him understand."

How am I supposed to do that, Jack thought, when I don't understand it myself? He nodded but stayed seated on the step and watched as his father headed down the walk, got into his car, and drove away.

It occurred to him that this was the most time he'd spent with his father in months.

All things considered, he figured, he'd take it.

11

The one sport Chris had never bothered with was boxing. And yet, she'd just managed a TKO. If Jack hadn't been standing across the room, he'd have sworn she'd given him an actual right cross to the chin.

And the irony was that she'd beaten him to the punch.

"Whadya mean, Sam asked you to the cotillion?"

"I mean," said Chris calmly, "that he invited me to be his date. Nitwit."

"I hope you told him you were already going with me. I asked you first." It was a ridiculous line, considering what he'd come over to tell her.

"Of course I told him you asked me. Then he

asked me to ask you, since you and I were just going as friends, if you wouldn't mind if I went with
him."

The fact that Jack already had a date with Emily
didn't stop him from demanding, "And who am I supposed to go with?"

"Forget it," she said, her voice reasonable. "I don't
have to go with him. I already promised you—"

"Don't flatter yourself, Chris."

"I'm not flattering myself, Jack. All I meant was—"

"You meant you were going to do me a big favor
and be my date."

"The only favor I'm doing you, Jack, is that I'm re-
fraining from beating the daylights out of you right
now, for acting like such a dope!" Chris closed her
eyes, taking a deep breath to regain composure. "Look
. . . I said I'd go to the dumb dance with you, and in
the seven years I've known you, neither of us has ever
broken a promise to the other, so I'm not about to
start now, especially over some idiotic upper-crust
mating ritual like a summer cotillion, okay? I only
mentioned it because Sam's really nice, and I thought
maybe you wouldn't care one way or the other."

He was hoping she'd add something along the lines
of "and because, given your new popularity status
with the in crowd, I knew you'd have no trouble finding a real date to take my place." But she didn't.

He settled on the first response he could think of. "I *don't* care. One way or the other."

"Fine."

"Fine."

"Good." She narrowed her eyes at him. "You're such a jerk, Jack."

"I'm a jerk? You're the one who—"

"Save it, Jack. I know you already agreed to go with Emily."

That shut him up. He stared at her. "How did you know?"

"Please, Jack. She told all her little groupies the minute you said yes. Kara told me, because she had a hunch you'd asked me first, and she didn't want me to hear it from Emily."

Jack's anger turned immediately to guilt, and he lowered himself onto a chair near one of the tall windows. Below, Main Street was all but deserted.

"So I guess Kara thinks I'm a dirtball, huh?"

"Actually, she thinks that you're sort of terrific but you've temporarily fallen under Emily's evil spell." Chris gave him a slow smile. "I'm inclined to agree."

Jack sighed. "So you knew I was gonna bail on you, but you still wouldn't say yes to Sam until after you talked to me."

Chris shrugged. "I owed you one . . . for buying the tampons."

Jack laughed in spite of himself. "This doesn't even begin to cover *that* debt!"

"Whatever."

"Can I ask you somethin'?"

"Sure."

"What was with that glamorous little tennis getup?"

She grinned. "I wouldn't exactly call it glamorous, Jack. Adorable, possibly. Even sweet. But glamorous? I don't know, *glamorous* sort of implies satin. And strapless. Maybe some sequins goin' on somewhere . . ."

"Okay, okay. So what was with the *adorable* getup?"

For a moment, Chris's eyes seemed fixed on the view through the window. When she finally spoke, she looked straight at him. "I didn't want to embarrass you."

His chin dropped.

"Remember last time? Those old ladies were looking at me funny."

Jack remembered.

"I got it on sale at that tennis shop Amy likes . . . Net Worth, you know. Anyway, I thought it would help me blend in a little better."

Jack was genuinely moved by the gesture. She'd gone against the grain to protect his status at the club. "You must have been miserable."

"Actually, it wasn't all that bad. I mean, it was just clothes."

"Clothes and makeup," Jack reminded her, with a grimace.

Chris rolled her eyes. "Yes, I know your position regarding me in mascara. But I didn't exactly mind that either. It was weird. I think I felt safer when I was wearing it. Like shoulder pads for my face."

Jack gave her a look that told her he thought she'd lost her mind.

"I know it sounds ridiculous, but it's true. You know those football players aren't really that big, but their pads make them look like they are. Everyone's shoulders look about the same size, which helps."

"Helps *what*? Shoulder pads aren't eye shadow, Chris."

"You don't get it."

"Yeah, well," Jack mumbled, "a week ago, you wouldn't have gotten it either."

A gleam of understanding lit in her eyes, but she didn't say anything regarding what she understood. That was fine with Jack; he wasn't sure he wanted to know.

Smiling, she sank into the chair beside him—on *top* of him, more or less—and dropped her head onto his shoulder.

Girlish. In the extreme.

Jack felt his shoulders go tense. Chris was practically on his lap. It wasn't an entirely unpleasant position to be in, once you got past the brain-shattering weirdness of it.

And, of course, his eyes picked that moment to land on her legs.

They were the same legs he'd seen but not noticed yesterday, when she was wearing that tennis skirt. But here, today, lying long and firm alongside his own, they were impossible to miss.

"I gotta go."

"What? Don't tell me you're still mad."

"No. No, I'm not mad. I'm just . . ." *on the verge of spontaneously combusting.* "Uh . . . hungry."

"Then let's go across the street and grab some doughnuts."

"Chris!"

"What?"

"Just get off my lap."

"*What*? I am *not* on your *lap*."

Jack squirmed. "What would you call it, then?"

"I'd call it sitting next to my best friend."

"Next to? Try another preposition. Like *atop*, maybe."

"Are you nuts?"

Maybe he was. He had no idea why Chris sitting close to him would make him feel so weird. Heck, how many times had they wrestled each other to see who got to choose which video to rent? And what about all those times they'd fallen asleep lying together in the hammock in his backyard? How was this suddenly different?

"I am *not* 'atop' you, Jack!"

"How does *astride* grab you, then?"

"*Astride?*" She sprang to her feet. "Don't be gross!" I couldn't have been less 'astride' you if I tried! And another thing . . . don't go throwing prepositions around with me, okay, because if it wasn't for me, you wouldn't know a preposition from a pronoun, or an adverb from an adjective!"

His fury ignited, fueled mostly by his overwhelming confusion about why he was even mad at all. He catapulted out of the chair. "Yeah, well, you can just . . . kiss my adjective! You and your new pretty-boy, prep-school boyfriend." He glared at her. "How do you like them adverbs, sweetheart?"

At that, Chris planted her hands on her hips and began stalking him around the room. "Sweetheart? So now that you're one of the Beautiful People, you can't just call me by my name anymore?"

"Sure, I can call you by your name . . . Christy!"

She stopped in her tracks, glowering at him, her nose an inch from his own. Four, maybe five hundred years of fiery silence passed before she spoke again. "Get out."

Jack didn't need to hear it twice. In fact, he didn't think he could live through hearing it twice. Without a word, he turned, stomped down the stairs and out of the apartment.

Leaving Christy, and her beautiful legs, behind.

Jack needed to talk.

He also needed a haircut, so the opportunity lent itself nicely. He swung open the door to Hot Rollers and stepped inside.

It had been two days since he'd been anywhere near Main Street, and, to his recollection, he'd never walked into Hot Rollers without Chris.

Soxie looked up from her client's nails and paused in her polishing to frown at him.

Well, he decided, that would certainly save time; if Soxie knew about his fight with Chris, then Mr. Moffett knew as well. Jack could skip all the explanation and jump right to the advice part. He approached the receptionist with a smile.

"I'd like a haircut, please."

The girl snapped her gum at him and checked the appointment book. "Desiree's free."

"Oh. Uh . . ." Jack glanced toward the back of the salon, where Chris's dad was using a curling iron to put the finishing touches on some lady's hairdo. As far as Jack could tell, Mr. Moffett hadn't noticed him. "I was hoping to get Nick."

The receptionist glanced over her shoulder. "Be about ten minutes."

"Thanks."

Jack took a seat on the banquette and absently reached toward the magazines scattered across the glass coffee table—*Cosmo*, *Mademoiselle*, *Marie Claire*, *Elle*. Not his usual reading preference, but he knew if he didn't have something to look at, he'd wind up staring at Soxie. He settled for *Mademoiselle*, because of all of them its cover model was wearing the least revealing outfit.

He flipped a few pages, taking in the ads. One included a folded-over strip, which he opened; the smell of expensive perfume nearly asphyxiated him. He quickly tried to reseal it, but that only made matters worse, since the scent was now stuck to his fingers.

Jack scowled as he turned the pages. He decided that if alien beings ever got hold of one of these magazines, they'd probably surmise that lipstick was a necessary component of human existence. How could they imagine otherwise? Any product that provided "thirty-four hot, new, must-have colors for fall" certainly sounded like a necessity.

In one ad, the picture of the lipstick tube was blown up to be almost as big as the model's face. The model herself was pouting for the camera (putting Emily's pout to shame), her lips coated with the supershine, moisture-release formula, which in Jack's opinion was a very unnatural shade of bluish purple. According to the ad, the color was called Vibrant Violet, but Jack didn't see anything vibrant about it. The purple color made it look as though she were freezing to death.

On the next page, a competitor's lipstick model was wearing Plum Pucker. Still purple, Jack decided. And four pages later, another ad, this one for lip color with a Miracle Stay-On Formula, was pushing a shade called Grape Expectations.

Purple. All of them.

Somewhere in the back of his mind, Jack made a connection—with football shoulder pads.

"Jack?"

He dropped the magazine. "Hi, Mr. Moffett."

"Need a trim?"

"Uh, yeah."

Mr. Moffett pointed to the sink. "Have a seat. Jennifer'll give you a wash."

Jennifer turned out to be almost as cute as Soxie. She leaned over him, and Jack wondered how much shampoo she'd have to use in order to wash the dirty thoughts he was having right out of his head. Her fingers on his scalp felt amazing—too amazing—and he was glad when the wash was over.

She escorted him to Mr. Moffett's chair and draped a nylon cape around him. Jack smiled at her in the mirror. She gave his damp hair a little tousle and left.

"So . . ." said Mr. Moffett, coming up behind the chair and spinning his scissors on his thumb. His reflection took up most of the mirror. "What are we doing today? Just cleaning up the ends?"

"I guess."

Mr. Moffett grinned. "No drastic changes, then?"

"Nope." Something in the grin made Jack wonder if the guy was talking about more than just hair. He lowered his chin and let Chris's dad make a few careful snips at the back of his neck. "How's Chris?"

"Grouchy." Mr. Moffett took a comb from the shelf beneath the mirror. "I think this is the longest you two have ever gone without talking. Am I right?"

He was, not counting the time Jack got his tonsils out and *couldn't* talk.

"I guess she told you about the cotillion."

"Yep."

Jack stared at the wrinkles of the nylon cape for a

moment, then lifted his eyes to meet Mr. Moffett's in the mirror. "You must think I'm a real jerk, huh?"

"Yep." He gave a little shrug. "Which would make us even, wouldn't it?"

Jack gulped; the morning Mr. Moffett had come in from the previous evening's date! So the guy *had* sensed his disapproval. For a fleeting moment, Jack worried the haircut might result in a Mohawk.

But Mr. Moffett chuckled. "You were right, you know. It was an irresponsible thing for me to do. I *was* a jerk."

Jack relaxed beneath the cape.

Mr. Moffett lifted a lock of hair between two fingers and cut it on an angle. "To tell you the truth, though, it wasn't the broken date that bothered her so much as that whole lap incident."

Jack's eyes widened. "She told you that?"

Mr. Moffett cut another angular slice off the top. "Don't worry. I know it was innocent."

"Innocent," Jack muttered. "But uncomfortable." He scowled.

"I can imagine. In fact, I defended you on that charge. I told Chris that she should cut you some slack, since it's not every day a guy finds a beautiful girl in his arms."

"What did she say?"

"She said she *wasn't* in your arms. Or on your lap."

Mr. Moffett came around in front of Jack and examined a long section of hair near his left ear. "Yet another example of how differently men and women can interpret a situation."

"I don't get it," Jack said, sighing. "It's like, she's this totally different kid all of a sudden. She's playing tennis with guys . . ."

"Guys other than you, you mean . . ."

"Yeah. And now she's got legs."

"I seem to recall Chris always having legs. But I know what you mean." Mr. Moffett laughed. "Could it be that the fact that you're just realizing it means you're suddenly a different kid yourself?"

"Maybe," Jack conceded.

"Changes are part of a relationship, Jack. Especially when you've known someone since before they got their permanent teeth."

"Teeth are one thing," Jack said solemnly. "Legs are another."

Again, Mr. Moffett grinned. "Couldn't have said it better myself."

"So what do I do? Stop asking her to shag fly balls, and start asking her to sit on my lap?"

"Do you *want* her to sit on your lap?" Mr. Moffett snipped at Jack's sideburns, smiling. "And please, don't let the fact that I'm holding a pair of razor-sharp scissors influence your answer."

Jack considered the question. "No. At least I don't think I do." He hesitated. "Do you think *she* wants to sit on my lap?"

"Tough call."

Tell me about it, thought Jack. "She's the one who's changing. I'm just . . . reacting to the changes."

"Badly, I'd say." Mr. Moffett raked his fingers through Jack's bangs. "Why is that?"

"Why? Well, because I liked her the way she was."

"Don't like her now?"

"Of course I like her. I just don't understand her, that's all."

"Not as well as you understand Emily Baskin."

"I *don't* understand Emily. *Nobody* understands Emily."

Mr. Moffett shook off the clippings that clung to his fingers. "Sam and Kyle don't seem to mind the changes."

Jack rolled his eyes. "That's an understatement!"

"So maybe it's not Chris changing that bothers you, Jack."

"What do you mean?"

Mr. Moffett was quiet for such a long moment that Jack thought he wasn't going to answer. He combed Jack's hair straight back. Then he combed it all over to the left. Then to the right. "You know what I did for a living before Chris was born?"

Jack didn't.

"I was a construction worker. You know those sweaty guys you see working on the highway all the time?"

Jack nodded. Amy loved to honk the car horn at those guys—when Cuff wasn't in the car, of course.

"That was me," said Mr. Moffett. "Road repair. Then one day, when my wife was pregnant with Chris, she asked me to drive her to the hairdresser's, because, at that point, she was too enormous to fit behind the wheel. So, of course, I take her, and I'm sitting there in the waiting area, watching, and there's this woman in one of the chairs—she's maybe the size of a reasonably large elf, okay? And she's got this *hair* . . . like six or seven hundred pounds of hair, and it's everywhere! Flipping back, and curling under and tumbling halfway down her back. You get the picture. And I'm thinking, This woman has got to go shorter. Much shorter. She's way too tiny to pull off that kind of style, she needs something wispy." He met Jack's eyes in the mirror. "Jack, until that moment, I didn't even know I knew the word *wispy*. But you know something?"

"What?"

"I was right. Her stylist whipped out these scissors and started chopping. Chopping and slicing and snipping, and the next thing I knew, there was the exact haircut I'd imagined for her. And it looked great. It looked amazing. In fact, I couldn't take my eyes off the woman . . . as my extremely pregnant wife pointed out to me afterward."

"So you decided to give up road repair and go in for hair repair?"

"You got it. Enrolled at the beauty academy the next day. All my construction buddies thought I was nuts. On the job, they'd call me Vidal Sassoon, and ask me when they could make an appointment."

Jack felt awkward about the next question, since he knew it always made Chris sad to talk about her late mom. But he had to know. "What did your wife think?"

Mr. Moffett hestitated, ostensibly to check the position of Jack's part. "She trusted me," he said at last.

"I don't get it."

"She knew I was making a big change—but she trusted me." He unsnapped the back of Jack's cape, removing it with a tug. "And she was right."

Jack studied his haircut in the mirror; it was flawless.

"I do trust Chris," he said softly. "I just don't want to lose her."

Mr. Moffett put a hand on Jack's shoulder. "You won't. You can't."

"But Sam . . . and Kyle . . ."

"They don't want what you have. What they want . . ."

Chris's dad stopped short with a frown that was only half-teasing. "Well, that's *my* problem to worry about."

Jack laughed. Then the sound of the door opening made them both turn.

Chris.

Chris, smiling, lugging a huge shopping bag through the door; behind her, Amy's car was pulling away from the curb.

Soxie was already across the salon, asking to see what Chris had bought. That was when Chris saw Jack. Her smile vanished. "I'll show it to you upstairs," she said stiffly, backing out the door.

Jack's stomach lurched. It didn't take a genius to figure out what was in that bag.

It was the dress she didn't buy to wear to the dance with him. The dress she bought to wear for Sam.

Mr. Moffett knew it, too. "Haircut's on me, kid," he said gently.

But, of course, that really didn't help at all.

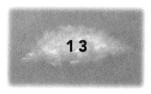

13

Amy was sworn to secrecy.

"Can you at least tell me what color it is?"

She shook her head. "Forget it."

Jack threw up his hands in exasperation. The churning in his stomach that had begun when Chris left the hair salon was increasing steadily. He knew he should probably eat something—but in the two days since he'd fought with Chris, he just hadn't been able to dredge up much of an appetite.

He crossed the family room and dropped onto the sofa. "I'm just asking for the color."

"And I'm just saying I won't tell you."

Jack groaned. He needed to know what shade Chris

was wearing to the dance so he'd be sure to include the right color pencil in his arsenal. As long as he was going to be sketching cotillion night portraits, his erstwhile best friend might as well be one of his subjects. Emily would probably be jealous, but it was the only thing he could think of to get back in Chris's good graces.

"Amy . . ."

"No, Jack! The answer is no." She looked up at him from where she knelt on the floor beside her model, pinning the hem of her own dress. "And for Lord's sake, Jack. Get some sleep. You look awful!"

Jack couldn't argue. He did look crummy—pale and miserable. He'd slept even less than he'd eaten over the last couple of days, and it was catching up with him. There was a ringing sensation in his head that suddenly made him feel dizzy.

He struggled to keep his eyes focused as he watched Amy fold up a section of the shimmery material, and he wondered how accurate the alterations were going to be. The bodice sagged in the chest area, because of the model's nonexistent bustline. Amy hadn't even attempted to zip up the back of the dress; it gaped open a good nine inches, and still the side seams were straining. The problem, of course, was that even though Amy's makeshift dummy was exactly her height, he weighed close to a hundred and ninety pounds.

Jack had to say this much, however—Cuff did look smashing in lavender.

"Stand still, honey," Amy urged, slipping a straight pin through the fabric.

"I'm trying." Cuff pawed at the skirt of the dress. "This crinoline's a killer." He tugged at the spaghetti strap that was creeping down his shoulder and glanced at Jack. "This makes my butt look big, don't it?"

Jack shrugged.

"If you cared so much about what Chris was wearing," said Amy, standing up and adjusting the other strap, "why did you break your date with her?"

"I didn't break it, because it was never really a date to begin with."

Amy planted her hands on her hips. "Did you invite her to go?"

His head throbbed. "I guess, but . . ."

"*With* you?"

"Yeah, but . . ."

"Then it was a date, Jack. Officially, legally, spiritually . . . you asked the girl out."

"The whole thing was an act of desperation. And she didn't even want to go in the first place."

Cuff smoothed the waistline, cocking his head at his

reflection in the French door. "These gathers are sort of flattering, though."

"You asked her, Jack, and you ditched her for Emily."

"She ditched me for Sam!"

"She checked with you first. Technically, that can't be considered ditching."

"I definitely see this with sandals," said Cuff. "Not pumps. No way."

Jack's head spun. "Just tell me what she's wearing!" he pleaded, through the increasing dryness of his mouth.

"Never."

Lukas appeared in the doorway. "What's going on?" He eyed Cuff. "Who are you supposed to be? Professional Wrestler Barbie?"

Cuff straightened his shoulders and sniffed. "I'm assisting with the alterations."

Lukas turned to his brother. "Hi, Jack."

"Hey, Lukey."

Lukas sat in an overstuffed chair that made him look very small. "Mom told me to make sure nobody goes anywhere." He paused to pick up Amy's pincushion from the coffee table. "We're going to have some big family meeting."

Jack felt his heart thump. "Meeting? What kind of meeting?" The words *custody battle* screamed in his head.

Amy looked as though she was thinking the same thing. "What else did she say, Luke?"

Lukas shrugged. "Just that we're having a meeting."

"*Who's* having a meeting?"

Lukas rolled his eyes and sighed as if the answer should have been obvious. "All of us. Me, you two, Mom, and Cuff, too, I guess. He's sort of family. If he takes off the dress."

"Anyone else?" Jack's queasiness increased tenfold.

"She didn't say," Lukas reported. "Maybe she's inviting the decorator over, since he may be family someday, too."

"You never know," said Amy.

Jack was about to contradict her when the doorbell rang. His first thought was that maybe it was Chris, and he sprang up from the sofa. Unfortunately, his brain hadn't gotten the "spring" command to his knees fast enough, because they nearly buckled with the effort. For a split second, a curtain of darkness threatened, but Jack blinked hard and the light returned.

"It's the decorator!" called Lukas, heading for the door. Amy and Cuff were right behind him. Jack did his best to keep up.

When they reached the foyer, though, Mom was already standing there with her hand on the doorknob.

"Don't let him in!" Lukas practically screeched.

Mom looked at him like he was crazy, then she opened the door.

But the handsome man waiting a little nervously on the front porch was not the interior decorator.

He was Dad.

A surge of hope made Jack momentarily forget his nausea. Maybe their father was moving back. But hope was quickly eclipsed by terror. There were no suitcases, nothing to indicate that Dad was home to stay. Maybe he was here to help Mom break the horrific news that they'd decided to get a full-fledged divorce.

Jack had to lean against the wall to steady himself. His eyes strained, and his stomach swirled. For a long moment, the only sound was the swish of Cuff's satiny gown.

Then Lukas spoke again.

But this time, Jack couldn't make out the words. Suddenly, he felt as if he were watching his brother through a dense fog. Lukas's lips were moving, but Jack heard only the pounding at his own temples.

The last thing he remembered was his mother turning to face him, but the movement seemed heavy and dreamlike to Jack. He had only enough time to notice the flicker of worry on his father's face and a glance shared between his parents.

Then came the thud, which he half felt, half heard,

since it was his own head hitting the floor, and after that, the very odd sensation that he was simply disappearing from the face of the earth.

At that particular moment, he almost wished he were.

Jack missed the meeting.

It was the second thought he had when he came to. His first was that Chris was standing over his bed.

There was something one-dimensional about her, though, and as he blinked his eyes into focus, he realized it wasn't Chris the person but Chris the drawing—one of his older ones, tacked to the wall near the bed.

He closed his eyes against the disappointment, hoping the blackness would sweep him away again. But a broad presence across the room caught his blurred attention.

The presence spoke. "You okay?"

"I think so."

Cuff sighed and came to sit on the edge of the bed. "Luke said you ain't been sleeping or eating since you and Chris had that fight."

Jack gave only a fleeting thought to denying it. "I haven't."

"Idiot."

No point arguing with that, he decided. Besides, more important issues were plaguing him at the moment; slowly, the scene in the foyer was coming back.

"What happened?"

Cuff adjusted the folds of Amy's cotillion dress. "You mean the meeting?"

Jack nodded.

"It's going okay, actually." Cuff took a deep breath and let it out slowly. "They're still talking downstairs. They basically said that they know it's been nuts around here, and that they aren't giving up yet."

"Funny, Dad moving out looked a heck of a lot like giving up to me."

"They're trying, Jack," said Cuff. "They're talking, and they said they're seeing some kind of counselor. They want to work things out." Cuff shrugged. "If you ask me, that's half the battle."

Jack gave his pillow a punch. "I wonder if Mom would want to work things out if she knew about Melissa."

"Who's Melissa?"

"Dad's girlfriend."

Cuff looked surprised. "That never came up at the meeting."

"Of course it didn't," Jack muttered. "Why would he confess?" He paused, scowling. "I bet she's gorgeous."

"Who?"

"Melissa," snapped Jack. "I mean, Dad wouldn't chuck his whole life for a dog, right?"

Cuff was silent.

Jack sighed. The faint had left a fuzzy residue in his mind; through it came a lipstick-on-linen image of Kara; absently he wondered if it had held up in the laundry. "It's pretty that does it."

Cuff gave him a crooked smile. "Does it for me."

"That's not what I meant." Jack sat up warily. "Being pretty can make a girl nasty. Selfish. It can mess up everything."

Cuff raised his eyebrows. "Who told you that?"

"Nobody had to tell me. Look around. Pretty girls are trouble."

"Amy's pretty. She ain't trouble."

Cuff's tone dared Jack to argue. Jack wasn't about to. Even in a dress, Cuff could easily squash him like a bug.

"All I know is that, whoever this Melissa is, she's probably a knockout, because if she wasn't, my parents wouldn't need to be talking to some stupid counselor."

"And if Chris wasn't pretty, she would be sitting here instead of me"—Cuff adjusted an unruly spaghetti strap—"right?"

"Right. I mean . . . no. Wrong. This has nothing to do with Chris."

"I think it does."

Jack pushed his hands through his hair in frustration. "Why can't it just be the same around here? Everything used to be great before. I knew what to expect."

"From your parents? Or from Chris?"

"Huh?"

Cuff leaned back against the footboard and sighed. "I think," he said patiently, "you're confusing your feelings about your parents splitting up with how you feel about what's going on between you and Chris." Cuff shook his head knowingly. "Chris changing, or Chris staying the same, has nothing to do with what's happening to your folks."

For a moment, Jack just stared at him. Cuff was a caveman; since when did he have insights? Good ones, no less?

Maybe it had something to do with the dress.

"I told you it has nothing to do with Chris."

Cuff shrugged. "I think it does."

Jack opened his mouth to disagree, but the certainty in Cuff's expression stopped him. He felt a sudden stranglehold in his chest, a tightness he didn't recognize. The truth seemed to wrap itself around his heart, a smothering honesty, defying Jack to disclaim it.

But he couldn't. Cuff was right. For Jack, the problem wasn't just that his family was dissolving before his eyes—the problem was that Chris wasn't going to be the same while it did.

Cuff was quiet a moment, studying his fingernails. Jack half expected him to ask what color polish he should wear with the dress.

"You'd think you'd be happy for her," he said at last.

"Happy?"

"Yeah. Happy. She's your best friend, isn't she? Or is she only your friend when she's beating you at HORSE?"

"That's my point, Cuff. There isn't going to be any more HORSE. Because now there's Sam. And lip gloss. And those darn legs."

"Listen, Jack." Cuff stood up and looked around at the drawings of Chris on the wall. "You can't do that to her, okay? You can't just pin Chris to your wall and keep her there, exactly like you want her to be, exactly like you remember her. It's not her job to keep your life together."

"But it is her job to be there while it's falling apart."

"What makes you think she isn't? She can be beautiful, Jack, and still be there." He took hold of the satin skirt and shook it at Jack. "If somebody ever told me I'd be doing this for Amy, I'd have told 'em they was nuts. Well, first, I'd have knocked their lights out, then I'd have told 'em they was nuts. But the point is . . . I love Amy. So I do this stupid stuff for her, because when you're in love, sometimes you do stuff you never thought you would. That's love. That's friendship, too. You go with the moment, and sometimes you go over the top. But love is over the top, Jack. And that's what makes it real."

"So I'm supposed to do something insane for Chris?"

"Yeah, you are."

"And what is it I'm supposed to do?"

"Trust her."

Jack frowned and fell back into the pillows. That's what Mr. Moffett had said.

"How can I trust her, when I don't even recognize her?"

Cuff shrugged. "Sometimes, you just have to look at a person and say, 'I'll always know you, no matter what, even when I don't know you.' And sometimes, you wind up wearing a prom gown, and you know what?" He paused to smile down at the dress. "It almost doesn't even bother you to do it."

"And how is Chris gonna notice my insane stuff over Sam's insane stuff? And Kyle's?"

"Well," said Cuff, his skirt swaying as he headed for the door, "I guess that's up to you, Jack."

Jack sighed.

"I got to get back to Amy. The cotillion's in three days, and she's got to finish this hem."

"Right."

"Later, Jack."

"Later, Cuff."

When the door closed, Jack faced the wall and studied the picture he thought had been Chris. But the thought of her was so exhausting that Jack rolled over and went straight to sleep.

In his dreams, he enjoyed the spoils of new popularity, the most salient of which was his impending date with Emily.

A little while later, his father woke him. "I wanted to say . . . I mean, I need to tell you . . ."

Jack's sleepy voice was harsh. "Good-bye?"

"No. Not good-bye. We're trying to work things out, Jack. Your mom and I both just need some space right now. It just might take a while."

Jack sat up and leaned against the headboard but wouldn't meet his father's eyes. "And how does Melissa feel about that?"

His father looked confused. "She's fine with it. In fact, she's been very helpful."

Jack's eyes flashed. "That's sick! How can you even say that?"

His father lowered his brows at Jack. "Jack—who exactly do you think Melissa is?"

"Sh-she's . . ." Jack stammered. "I found her phone number in your shorts pocket at the club. She's your new girlfriend." He blinked. "Isn't she?"

"No!"

For a moment, Jack thought his father might actually laugh.

"Jack, Melissa is the family therapist your mom and I have been seeing. I guess I had her number in my pocket so I could call her from the club to schedule our next appointment."

Jack blinked again. He didn't know whether to feel relieved or embarrassed.

"I can't promise you this is going to have a completely happy ending, Jack. All I can promise you is that your mother and I are going to try. And no matter what happens, we'll always be a family. Even if things change, we'll still be a family."

Jack didn't know what to say, so he didn't say anything. He let his father place an awkward kiss on his forehead and watched him leave.

14

Jack had a theory about bow ties.

He figured they'd gone out of style among the social elite, not based on the dictates of fashion but rather in response to an increased divorce rate within that particular segment of the population. In other words, with dads out of the house, sons wouldn't have the faintest idea of how to tie a bow tie.

He'd been standing in front of the full-length mirror in his parents'—correction, his *mother's*—bedroom, struggling with the stupid accessory for what seemed like hours. Amy might have been able to assist, but she'd already left; she and Cuff were double-dating with Chris and Sam.

Frowning, Jack decided he'd let his date take a shot

at the tie on their way to the dance. In the *limousine*. That thought cheered him—riding through that gate, with none other than Emily Baskin, and waving to Kirby the guard from the backseat of the stretch limo her father had reserved for the night. Even Kirby would have to be proud of him for that!

He stepped backward to admire his reflection. Bow tie aside, he looked pretty neat in the black trousers and cream-colored dinner jacket.

"Jack?"

He adjusted his cuffs and turned to his mother in the doorway.

Her smile seemed a little brighter than the weepy one she'd been giving him since the day after his father had left. "You're positively dashing."

"Thanks."

"I wish you had come down to see Amy off. She looked beautiful. And Cuff—"

Jack shrugged, cutting her off. He'd stayed upstairs purposely, to avoid seeing Chris. They still weren't speaking; it was going to be bad enough seeing her at the dance. Watching her pose for pictures with Sam in Jack's own living room would have been beyond uncomfortable. That should have been apparent to his mother, but then again, she wasn't thinking clearly lately.

"I have something for you," she said, reaching into the back pocket of her jeans.

"What is it?"

She handed him a handsome leather case, about the size of a paperback book. Jack looked at it curiously, extending his hand.

"It's not from me," she said softly. "It's from . . . Dad."

His gaze snapped up to meet hers. "Dad?"

She nodded. "He sent a corsage for Amy, and this for you."

Jack withdrew his hand as if the case were an explosive device. "I don't want it."

"Yes, you do."

Jack shook his head.

His mother sighed and placed the case on the bed. "I know your date's on her way, so this probably isn't the best time to discuss—"

"You're right. It's not."

"Just hear me out, will you?"

"Mom . . ."

"Jack . . . listen. I need to say this, all right?" She lowered herself to the bed, taking a seat beside the mysterious gift from his father. "I owe you an apology."

Jack scowled in confusion.

She surprised him with chuckle. "I was a few sandwiches short of a picnic for a while there."

He considered pretending he didn't know what she

was talking about but decided against it. "You have been pretty distracted."

"Yes, I have."

"Do you still love each other?"

She nodded. "But it's more complicated than that."

Jack didn't see how it could be. And he didn't want to start thinking about it now.

Mom tapped the leather case with her finger. "I think you should take this. Even if you're angry with him, I've always believed there are two things a person should never let go unappreciated. One"—she slid the case across the bedspread toward Jack—"is a gesture of goodwill."

"What's the other?"

"A designer leather item."

Jack laughed, leaned down, and picked up the case. In the driveway, a car horn sounded.

"I imagine that's your date," said Mom, standing and heading for the door. "I'll tell her you'll be right down."

Jack hesitated, then gave the zipper a tug. The case fell open to reveal a collection of sixteen high-quality markers.

He remembered.

Jack studied the markers a moment, then closed the zipper and slipped the flat case into his pocket.

It was a neat gift, he decided, his fingers moving to

the still-undone tie at his throat. But as goodwill gestures went, he couldn't help thinking, it fell remarkably short.

Jack wondered how it had escaped him that Kyle's date was Kara. He was in the loop now, and yet he hadn't heard that. When he slid into the backseat of the Baskins' limo, he actually stared at her a moment, then told himself it was only because he hadn't been expecting to see her.

"Hi, Jack."

"Hi, Kara. Kyle."

Kyle appraised him coolly, offering a nod.

Jack turned to Emily and smiled in what he hoped was a charming manner. Her dress was a clingy black number that previous generations would have considered lingerie. "You look great."

"Whatever."

He mistook that for modesty. "No, really. I mean it. You look—"

"I said, *whatever*."

Embarrassed, Jack leaned back into the plush seat. He thought he noticed a fast look of disgust pass over Kara's face and wondered if it was for him or for Emily.

Kyle was looking a tad disgusted himself. "You forgot to tie your tie."

"Oh . . . no, actually, I didn't forget. I didn't know how."

Kyle snorted. Jack turned to Emily with an expectant grin.

"Sorry," she told him, sounding more insulted than apologetic. "Fresh manicure."

They drove in silence for a while.

Finding himself in sudden, desperate need of air, Jack hit the button to lower his window, just as the limo pulled up to the E.C.C. gate. The driver stopped to receive clearance from the guard, who was tipping his cap to the passengers.

"Mr. Jack Jordan," Kirby drawled, bending toward the window. "Good evening to you."

Jack smiled automatically at his friend. "Hi, Kirby."

"Begging your pardon, but I believe you've forgotten to tend to your tie."

"I know."

"Perhaps I could be of some assistance?"

Was it Jack's imagination, or was Kirby putting on a little show? His accent was suddenly thicker than usual, and his tone seemed sarcastically—what would be the word?—subservient. Jack shot a quick glance around the limo to see if any of the others seemed to notice. None of them did.

And the fact remained, he did need his tie tied. He gave Kirby a curious look, then lifted his chin. Kirby's gloved hands worked the odd-shaped strip of material deftly; in seconds, Jack's tie was knotted to perfection.

"Thanks, Kirb."

"My pleasure." Kirby raised his hand to his cap in a friendly salute. "You go on and enjoy yourselves."

As the car pulled through the gate, Jack turned to face his companions. Kara, he noticed, seemed a little surprised, but at least she was smiling. Kyle and Emily, on the other hand, looked thoroughly appalled.

"You know him?" asked Emily.

Jack shrugged. "Yeah." He felt his palms growing damp and fought the urge to wipe them on his trousers. "Don't you?"

"No," answered Emily, sounding half-amused, half-insulted. "Until just this second I didn't even know his name was Herbie."

"Kirby," whispered Kara.

"What . . . *ever*."

"He's a nice guy," Jack explained.

"He's the help," countered Kyle.

"Charlie the tennis pro is the help."

Emily let out a sigh of frustration. "That's different. Charlie's tennis. Corby—"

"Kirby."

"*Kirby* . . . is security. Actually, he's not even that." She wrinkled her nose. "He's traffic."

"He ties a mean bow tie, though," Kyle observed,

laughing, and Jack understood that it wasn't a charitable reference to Kirby but a scornful criticism of Jack.

The driver guided the car beneath the towering portico, then hopped out and hurried to open the rear doors.

Kyle took Kara's elbow and started off toward the entrance. Emily, though, was keeping an icy distance, so Jack just walked beside her.

When they reached the double doors, she turned to him abruptly. "Art supplies?"

In answer, Jack patted his pocket. And that was all it took. In a split second, she was plastered to his side, her arm linked in his, her smile a beaming masterpiece.

Jack smiled, too. Together, they made their entrance.

Eastport Country Club had never looked more magical.

The grand ballroom shimmered with soft light and the soft shades of dresses worn by laughing young ladies. The French doors that led to the veranda were open, allowing balmy night breezes to whisper in and swirl among the guests, who swirled among one another.

Jack, though, wasn't swirling.

Jack was sweating.

He sat at a table in the corner, surrounded by a small knot of onlookers. His head was bent over his canvas—a cocktail napkin—his seventh so far. He'd made the unfortunate mistake of forgetting to bring his sketchpad. It had taken Emily only a second to come up with the idea of snatching a stack of paper cocktail napkins from the bar. Jack felt bad about misusing club property—again—but at least this time the napkins were disposable. The thing was, the moment she'd provided the napkins, she'd disappeared. He'd been stuck behind the table drawing for nearly an hour, and she was nowhere in sight. The only reason he knew that she was still on the premises was the steady stream of "models" approaching him and saying, as though it were some secret password, "Emily said you'd draw me."

At the moment, he was working on a portrait of Millicent Rudgrove, the only thirteen-year-old member of Eastport Country Club who enjoyed more clout than Emily.

The pressure was unbearable. And all because of the bump.

Head-on, Millicent Rudgrove was beautiful—clear skin, bright eyes, masses of wavy auburn hair. Her profile, however, was another story, on account of a most unfortunate bump that protruded from the bridge of her nose.

Why it had never been fixed was one of the juiciest mysteries at Eastport. There were two rumors regarding the topic: one suggested that a prominent plastic surgeon had tried but failed to remove the bump, while the other proposed that Millicent was simply too chicken to go under the knife.

Jack's present dilemma was deciding whether to include the bump in his drawing, or to do a little artistic surgery of his own and leave it out. It was hard to guess which tactic would be the bigger insult.

There wouldn't have been a problem, he told himself for the hundredth time, if Millicent had just faced him for her sitting. But *no*, she insisted on turning her head to the side to engage in trivial conversation with some of the bumpless-nosed girls who were waiting to have their portraits done. So Jack had no choice but to sketch her in profile.

To bump, or not to bump? That was the question.

He picked up a blank cocktail napkin from the thick stack beside him and used it to wipe the perspiration from his forehead.

"Are you almost finished?" Millicent snapped. "I'd like to dance."

"I'm just . . . I'm almost . . ." The fact that there was no easy way to explain forced Jack to make his decision—teeth clenched, he finished Millicent's nose with a benevolently smooth line.

"It's done," he announced, handing over the cocktail napkin.

Millicent took the small, tissuey square and examined it. Jack kept his eyes low. Until he heard the coo.

That's what it was. A coo . . . an actual *coo* of satisfaction from Millicent. Jack looked up and saw that she was beaming over the drawing. She gave him a dazzling smile, and he wondered if she realized that the perfect nose in the drawing did not, in fact, carry over into real life, that she was, in reality, as bumpy as she'd been before the sketch.

"It's uncanny!" breathed Millicent, holding one corner gingerly between her thumb and forefinger so as not to smudge the colors. "It looks *exactly* like me."

Jack certainly wasn't about to debate it. He just sighed and watched Millicent float toward the dance floor to find her date.

"I'm next!" came Emily's voice from behind him. She was holding a glass of lemonade, and, for a moment, he thought she'd brought it for him. Fat chance. She took a long sip, then planted herself in the seat across from him. It occurred to Jack that it was the closest she'd been to him all evening.

Some date.

"Problem?" she asked. It sounded like a dare.

Jack shook his head.

"So draw, Picasso."

"Right." He took a deep breath and picked up his new flesh-toned marker to sketch the outline of her face.

He'd just finished the outline of her forehead when she spoke again.

"And it better be as good as Millicent's," she said through her teeth.

Jack gripped the marker. Talk about attitude. Suddenly, he was a whole lot less fond of Emily Baskin than he'd been the day she invited him to the club. *His* club. And that's when it hit him. The only reason she'd asked him to this dance—cotillion, *one* word—was to get him to provide the party favors by sketching her friends!

"It'll be better," he promised, and went to work.

After a few minutes, he announced, "Finished. And you know something? It looks just like you!"

Jack had never attempted the fine art of caricature before, but evidently he had a flair for it. In this portrait, Emily's slightly pointy chin took on the appearance of a steak knife, and he made her pinched nose look as if it had been clamped together with a clothespin. And as for her cheekbones—well, in this sketch, she resembled a chipmunk, storing nuts for the winter! He was even careful to get her shimmery, artificial hair color right, including the strategically placed platinum highlights *and* the dark roots.

He handed her the napkin. She took it, smiling, and looked at it. Then the smile vanished.

Jack opened his eyes wide. "Problem?" he asked innocently.

Emily glared at him. "I hate you!"

"Emily," said Jack, standing, "you don't even know me."

With that, he picked up the unused napkins and headed to the bar to return them. But before he even made it to the dance floor, he noticed a sudden ripple of interest at the opposite side of the room. Clearly, a late arrival. Clearly, someone worth looking at.

Heads turned, whispers were exchanged. Even Millicent Rudgrove paused in admiring her napkin to take notice. Jack turned to see, curious.

Or maybe not so curious. Because it was almost as if he *knew*.

Who is that?" someone near him was asking. "Is she a member?"

"Dressed like *that*?"

"She looks . . ."

"Incredible."

"Different."

"Incredibly different."

"She's with Sam. Sam looks great."

"Yeah, but *she* looks . . ."

"She looks . . ."

"How would you describe it?"

"I'm not sure. What's her name?"

"Misty, I think."

"Not Misty. *Christy*. Christy Something. Christy . . . Misfit?"

"Christy *Moffett*."

"Well, whatever her name is, she looks . . . incredible."

For a moment, Jack thought about finding the guy who'd made the misfit remark and flattening him. He felt a wave of dread as he tried to imagine what it was that Chris was wearing—something his fellow club members couldn't even describe. Was it too skimpy? Too see-through? Too obviously from the sale rack?

Jack craned his neck, but his view of Chris was blocked by other people, craning their necks, standing on tiptoe. Through the crowd, he spotted Kyle, gaping. Jack was surprised to find himself wondering where Kara was.

Cuff was visible now, sweeping in with Amy on his arm, and Jack could see part of Sam—his left shoulder, his *considerable* left shoulder. Chris must have been standing to Sam's right, because he still couldn't find her.

When Jack caught Amy's eye, she grinned at him across the room; relieved, he smiled back. If Chris's appearance had been unacceptable, Amy would not be smiling as calmly as she was now.

And then, as if by some divine intervention, the crowd on the dance floor seemed to part, to open itself, so that Jack could at last have a glimpse of what he'd been trying so desperately to see. His best friend. Chris Moffett. In her . . .

. . . running clothes?

Jack blinked. The girl was wearing her *running clothes*! Some of them, anyway—her favorite nylon warm-up pants, the shiny black Adidas ones, with the three white stripes down the sides. Those were definitely running clothes, and yet, the *way* she was wearing them—slung low around her slim hips—said otherwise. They'd become glamorous, somehow. Formal. Chris *made* them formal. Jack had never noticed the way they hugged her before—those stripes skidding down the outsides of her legs actually swerved!

And then there was the top. It was made of shimmering black crushed velvet, and it stopped just below her ribs, leaving her tummy bare. The thin strap around her neck left her shoulders and upper back bare, too. Jack wasn't sure, but he thought it was called a halter. No female in her right mind would run in that top.

Or in those shoes—strappy high heels that made her legs seem even longer.

She was wearing makeup. Not too much, but enough so that it had an effect. Her hair was swept up into a loose twist, with plenty of wispy spirals to frame her face. The style had a tangled elegance that could have taken hours, or seconds, to achieve. On her ears were a pair of glinting diamond earrings.

There were probably a hundred pairs of diamond earrings in the room, but there was only one pair of Adidas sweats. Statistically speaking, Chris should have felt awkward.

But, to Jack's amazement, it was not Chris who seemed inappropriate. It was all the other girls, in their long gowns and tea-length gowns and short gowns, who suddenly seemed self-conscious and shown up. He half imagined he could hear them wishing they'd been so creative, so daring, so utterly individual and cutting-edge trendy.

This was a trend that wouldn't even *become* a trend until tomorrow, when they could get themselves to the mall.

And it was Christy Not-Even-a-Member Moffett who'd started it!

Amy was approaching him now. Jack tore his eyes away from Chris to face her.

"Not a bad way to make an entrance, huh?" she said.

"Where the heck were you?"

"We went back to Cuff's house so his folks could play paparazzi." She grinned. "Chris looks amazing, doesn't she?"

"No wonder you were sworn to secrecy."

"Let's face it, Jack. Anyone can look ladylike in a floor-length sequined sheath. But it takes a unique person to look feminine in a pair of running pants."

Jack nodded. He wondered if Emily, or Millicent, or the others realized, as he did, that Chris was mocking them—beating them at their own game. She was doing their thing, *her* way . . . and doing it better.

He'd never been so proud of anyone.

And, suddenly, the rest of the night lay ahead like some perfect dream—with Chris making such a stunning debut, Emily might overlook the caricature and beg him to finish out the date. Not that *he* wanted to, but it would be nice to see her grovel.

In fact, she was approaching him right now.

But she didn't look as though she wanted to reconcile.

"Oooh," said Amy, smiling, "this looks interesting."

Emily was gripping something in her fist—her sketch, crumpled into a ball. She threw it at him. "Your social life is finished, you twerp," she hissed.

Jack almost laughed.

"And for your information, Kyle was the one who made me invite you to the pool in the first place. He's got this thing for your pal what's-her-name. The only reason I even paid attention to you was to keep you away from her so Kyle could make his move." Her eyes darted sideways toward where Chris was standing close to Sam. "Looks like we both wasted our time."

"Guess we did," said Jack. There were a hundred names he would have liked to call her, but deep down, he knew she wasn't worth the effort.

His sister, apparently, felt quite differently. "So, Emily, where'd you get your dress? Tramps-R-Us?"

Emily's mouth dropped open, but the only sound she could manage was an angry little squeak.

"Oh, and nice hair." Amy gave a disgusted snort. "I've done chem labs that didn't require that many chemicals. Uh, and one more thing . . . if you ever talk to my brother that way again, I'll knock every one of those capped teeth right out of your vicious little mouth."

At that, Emily's face went positively white. Without a word, she stomped off. When she was out of sight, Jack turned to Amy, who was calmly smoothing the gathers at her waistline.

"Wow."

Amy shrugged. "You just got to know how to handle 'em, Jack."

"Handle who?"

"Pretty girls." She gave him a wink. "They're trouble, you know."

"Not all of them," said Jack, leaning over to kiss his sister on her cheek.

They laughed; then Amy's expression became serious. "I guess you're on your own now."

"Guess so."

"You're welcome to hang around with Cuff and me, except I have a feeling we're going to be spending a lot of time on the dance floor."

Jack temporarily forgot his troubles, and his eyes widened. "Cuff? On the dance floor?"

"Yes!" Amy nodded. "For the last six weeks, he's been going to dance lessons! He did it as a surprise for me! Isn't that *insane?*"

Jack couldn't help smiling. "Yes," he agreed. "Perfectly insane."

"Well, I guess I'd better find him before he starts the fox-trot without me." She touched Jack's arm. "Will you be okay?"

"I'll be fine," he lied. "Go ahead."

Amy gave him another smile before disappearing into the crush of people. Just as he lost sight of her, he felt someone standing behind him. He didn't have to turn around to know who it was.

Maybe, he told himself, he'd be fine after all.

"You look terrific."

"You think?"

"Yeah. And it's not just me . . . everybody thinks so."

Chris scrunched up her nose. "I hate being stared at."

"You wouldn't hate being stared at if you were pitching a no-hitter."

"True."

"So just think of this as a no-hitter." Jack sighed. "I'm sure striking out."

"I heard."

"Already? From who?"

"Oh, well, let's see . . ." She held up her hand and began ticking off the batting order on her fingers. "Emily told Kyle, Kyle told Millicent's date, I forget his name . . . anyway, he told Millicent, Millicent told Kara, and Kara told me."

"Nobody told the maître d'?" mused Jack.

"Actually, I think the bartender did. By the way, the bartender said he wouldn't charge your dad's account for all the napkins you used if you'd do his portrait."

Jack sighed glumly. "So far, that's the best news of the night."

They were quiet a moment, watching the other couples dance. A few in particular caught Jack's attention: Jillian Montgomery and Drew Dayton, who, Jack knew for certain, were not romantically linked but, rather, the reigning junior mixed doubles champions;

Vanessa Kimball and Will Borden, who only tolerated each other because their fathers were law partners and they'd been thrown together since birth; Cole Corbett, who was actually dancing with his sister, Candace.

Jack acted on an impulse. "I don't suppose . . ." he began, just as Chris said, "You probably wouldn't want to . . ."

They looked at each other and laughed.

"Would you like to dance?"

"Sure."

"Will Sam mind?" Jack hoped he didn't sound as bitter as he felt.

"Of course not." Chris cleared her throat. "Actually, he's the one who sent me over here to talk to you."

The threat of humiliation prickled through Jack. "Why? Did he feel sorry for me?"

"Probably."

"Do you feel sorry for me?"

"Is this a trick question?"

"No. Really. I want to know."

She thought before she answered. "No," she said at last. "I don't feel sorry for you. Thinking you could have something with Emily was dumb, Jack. You were playing with fire, and you got burned, but it's not the end of the world."

Jack grimaced. The only thing that bothered him more than Super Sam taking pity on him was Chris *not* taking pity on him. But he wasn't about to admit it.

"So," she said. "Do we dance?"

"We dance."

They moved onto the floor, and Jack took her right hand while she placed her left one on his shoulder. As his right hand slid to her waist, he noticed that Sam was watching. Feel sorry for me now, pal? he thought, and pulled Chris a little closer.

On the opposite side of the dance floor, Sam shifted his weight anxiously.

Jack smiled to himself, closing his fingers tightly around Chris's. Out of the corner of his eye, he could see Sam closing *his* fingers tightly around his glass; the guy didn't look mad, but he did look worried.

Jack decided he preferred worried. Very casually, he leaned his forehead against Chris's.

"What are you doing?" she whispered.

"Dancing."

"I didn't know it was a contact sport," she teased. "I guess you're trying to make Emily jealous, huh?"

Jack didn't answer; in fact, he hadn't really heard the question. His thoughts were drifting back to the day Chris hadn't sat on his lap. That had been confusing, unsettling. But this was different. Comfortable. Maybe if instead of sitting next to him that day she'd asked him to dance, they'd never have had that argument.

He dropped his hand slightly, to her hip. She took a deep breath, which pleased Jack, because she sounded very content, and also because, for the space of a second, her whole torso skimmed his.

She was a good dancer, for a jock. And she smelled nice. One of her wispy curls was tickling his face. Her hair, his cheek.

Jack knew that when the song was over, Chris would go back to her date, who, at that very moment, was waiting nervously at the edge of the dance floor.

Let him, thought Jack. This is my dance.

Around them, girlfriends cuddled boyfriends, and blind dates agonized over where to put their hands, and friends and cousins and brothers and sisters made fun of each other for dancing so badly. It was a long song, a wonderfully long song.

Terror struck when it occurred to Jack that Sam could always cut in. If that happened, the polite thing would be for Jack to allow it.

And then she'd go.

In her sexy halter and running pants. She'd go.

His heart thundered, and he had a crazy image of himself scooping her up and taking off with her into the night.

But that would be dumb. Dumb again—dumb like falling for Emily Baskin, like fighting with Chris in the first place.

He hadn't lost her, though, not completely. She was here with Sam, but she was dancing with Jack . . . and Jack was dancing with her.

A thought struck him like lightning, followed by a thunder in his heart.

Perhaps he'd been wanting to dance with Chris Moffett all his life. Perhaps he'd been needing to, waiting to . . . planning to take her in his arms, like this, and hold her close. Like this.

He didn't *remember* planning it, but maybe, just maybe . . .

Then the song was fading, the dance ending, and, in the distance, Sam was ready to claim the next one. Jack's first instinct was to panic, but he knew that too would be dumb. He didn't want to waste one second on panic, he just wanted to enjoy these last few seconds so close to Chris.

But did they have to be the last?

Jack might have been dumb all along, but perhaps now he was finally going to be smart.

Maybe now it was time for him to fall in love with her.

Maybe he already had.

Jack followed Chris off the dance floor, to where Sam waited.

"Hi."

"Hi."

"Hi."

No one seemed to know what to say after that. Jack stuffed his hands into his pockets. Chris tugged at one of her earrings. Sam tapped at the rim of his glass.

Luckily, Millicent sailed over, and the uneasiness was drowned in her wake. She introduced herself to Chris and immediately began bubbling questions about her outfit, without ever actually admitting that she liked it.

"So where do you shop?" Millicent inquired, in an attempt at offhandedness. "Bloomingdale's? Bergdorf's?"

Unruffled, slipping her thumb into the elastic waistband of the pants and giving it a good snap, Chris named several local sporting-goods stores. "Sneaker Shack, Adams Athletics, Good Sports."

"Ohhhh." Millicent gave her a glowing smile, although she looked as if she'd rather give her a slap.

"Okay, so I was just sort of wondering . . . if you were going to, say, a garden party, say, for a Sweet Sixteen . . . what would you wear?"

Jack studied Chris's face, and he could tell it was taking all she had not to laugh out loud at Millicent's question.

"Well, now that depends," said Chris, her voice steady and serious, as if the fate of the world depended on this. "Is this a late-day affair? An afternoon-tea type get-together? Or is it early, you know, like a brunch?"

"Early," Millicent clarified. "It's an early luncheon."

"Hmm. Okay. Well, then, I'd definitely go with shorts."

"Shorts?"

"Yes, umm-hmm. Definitely. Shorts. The little nylon ones, like runners wear. Maybe in a pastel color, but not the kind with the drawstring in the waist, because the string always makes a bump in your middle."

Millicent nodded gravely, soaking up the information as if she were being entrusted with the very secrets of the universe.

"And on top . . . well, I think I'd do something really risky. Like maybe a lacy camisole, something totally glamorous, under a linen bolero jacket—no, wait, not linen . . . silk shantung. And forget about shoes—you have to go with sneakers. Real high-tech running sneaks, the kind with the reflective strips on them. That way, if you happen to catch the sunlight at just the right angle"—she paused, smiling exquisitely— "well, you might blind everyone, but at least you'll be the talk of the party."

By this point, Millicent was looking a little groggy, as if waking from some magical fashion dream. She nodded once more, then, without even thanking Chris for her input, she left, murmuring, "Sneaker Shack . . . not Bergdorf's . . . Good Sports . . ."

Sam and Chris exchanged smiles.

Then it got quiet again.

A waitress appeared with a tray of hors d'oeuvres— enormous shrimp, scallops wrapped in bacon, little toasted triangles smeared with something or other. In the center of the tray was a tiny crystal cup filled with toothpicks.

Sam helped himself to some shrimp, Chris opted for the toast concoction, and Jack used a toothpick to spear a fat scallop.

Chris was staring at Sam as though the guy's chewing were the most entertaining thing she'd ever witnessed in her life.

Hey! Remember me? The guy who just fell in love with you on the dance floor?

Another food server appeared. This time, Jack poked himself a plump little spring roll. Chris was too busy feeding off the vision of Sam standing there, swallowing shrimp.

Jack wondered grimly how many of those scrawny toothpicks he would need to kill himself—one through the heart, two more into his temples, maybe one poked into each eyeball. Of course, he'd probably get into trouble for wasting the club's toothpicks on something as insignificant as his suicide.

He knew his thoughts were in direct opposition to the mood of the event taking place around him. Chris tried to engage him in conversation once, asking if he had any gut feelings about who might win the U.S. Open. Jack couldn't venture a guess—didn't even care to, so Sam, proving himself to be intelligent on top of handsome, athletic, and just plain nice, slid gracefully into an entertaining discussion of last year's U.S. Open and the subsequent off-court antics of the men's champion.

Jack now found himself wondering how many toothpicks it would take to kill Sam.

One . . . if it were made of kryptonite.

When Sam asked Chris to dance, Jack nearly choked on his spring roll. Pretending not to notice, Chris accepted with a sparkling smile. Jack couldn't bring himself to watch.

He would have been forced to endure an entire set of slow songs, staring at the highly polished brass rail along the bottom of the bar, if it hadn't been for Kara.

"Hi, Jack."

He looked up from the rail. Emily Baskin, fortunately, was nowhere to be seen.

"Hi, Kara."

"I'd ask if you were enjoying the dance, but . . ." She smiled gently. "I think I already know the answer."

"I've had better nights," he admitted.

"So have I. Kyle's holed up in the coat-check room with some of his buddies, losing half his trust fund in a poker game."

Jack cracked a gloomy smile. "Well, you know what they say . . . unlucky in cards, lucky in love."

He was surprised, and pleased, to see that his remark brought a blush to her cheeks. He tried to remember what flaw he'd noticed about her that day at the pool . . . something about her nose being slopey, or ski-jumpish? Funny—it didn't look at all slopey tonight.

"Chris looks terrific," Kara was saying. "Doesn't she?"

Jack nodded.

"I mean, I shopped for two months for this dress, and practically lost my mind over finding the right shoes. But Chris . . ." She smiled, respectfully. "Wow. She just put everyone to shame—and the best part is, she made it look easy!"

Jack would have expected her to feel that Chris's apparent ease at blowing everyone's doors in was the worst part, not the best. It sounded as if Kara was genuinely rooting for Chris tonight. Silently, he scolded himself for expecting Kara to be so cutthroat—the truth was, he really didn't know her well enough to expect anything from her. He'd been confusing her with Emily, and was glad to learn that he'd been wrong.

"You look terrific, too," he said, wishing he'd mentioned it sooner.

"Thanks. So do you."

"Thanks." He smiled.

She smiled.

They were two of the clumsiest smiles ever smiled. Embarrassed, Jack turned to the dance floor.

He knew he should probably invite Kara to dance. In another place, another time, maybe he would have. But here and now it was just too complicated. All he really wanted was to be dancing with Chris, but she was dancing with Boy Wonder, who looked as if he had no immediate plans to relinquish her.

As if to prove this conjecture, a lanky guy with curly hair and wide shoulders sidled up to Sam and asked if he might cut in on the dance.

Jack knew that Sam was bound by an ancient code of gentlemanly conduct to allow it.

But Sam did *not* allow it.

Curly Hair looked highly insulted.

Sam didn't seem to care. Jack almost laughed.

In the next second, Chris was being accosted by a girl in a yellow dress, who was ignoring her dance partner to fawn over Chris. The girl's exuberant gestures and giddy expression told Jack that the conversation was centered on Chris's unique concept of taste.

Chris looked disgusted.

At the end of the song, Sam led her off the dance floor. They returned to where Jack and Kara were standing. Chris seemed pleased to see Kara, but having her there didn't make Jack feel any less like a fifth wheel.

"Listen," said Sam. "Why don't we get out of here?"

Jack lowered his eyes. "No, that's okay. You guys stay . . . I'll go."

"You don't understand," Sam told him. "We should all go. I don't know about you, but I hate these things. I only came because my mom was on the committee and she would have felt hurt if I didn't at least make an appearance." He turned to Chris. "Not that I didn't want to bring you tonight . . . I did. But I would have been happier taking you to a movie, or dinner. Or . . . I don't know . . . just going up to the high school to play some HORSE."

Jack's knees buckled. He hadn't realized it was possible to hate someone as much as he hated Sam at that moment.

"I wouldn't mind leaving," said Chris. "If one more person asks me if Adidas is coming out with an haute couture collection this fall, I think I'll scream." She turned to Kara. "Come with us."

Kara's eyes flickered briefly toward Jack, but she sighed and shook her head. "I can't. I came with Kyle. I should leave with him—even if he is acting like a jerk." She smiled warmly at Chris. "Maybe you can come to the club next week—as my guest. We can have lunch."

Chris nodded, returning the smile. "Sounds great. Except why don't we make it Randall Park pool? And you can be *my* guest."

"Even better," said Kara.

Jack, along with Chris and Sam, said good-bye to Kara, then watched her make her way across the room to join the rest of the girls whose dates had deserted them for the card game.

"So are we out of here or what?" asked Sam.

"Definitely," said Chris. "But how? Cuff drove us."

"Not a problem," said Sam. "We'll just walk down to the gatehouse. Kirby'll call us a cab."

Jack thought his jaw might drop. "What?"

"I said Kirby will help us out. He's . . ."

"I know," said Jack, "the guard."

Sam nodded. "Great guy. I got stuck here without a ride one rainy day, and while I was waiting for my mom to pick me up, I hung out in the guardhouse with him. He taught me how to play backgammon."

Jack couldn't believe it—he didn't want to believe it. This guy played backgammon with the help—and enjoyed it.

Could this night get any worse?

He made his decision then and there. He was going to have to keep Chris as far away from Sam as possible. Then he'd show her how he felt. He'd win her back, he was certain. After all, he had seven years of best friendship going for him. Talk about a home-court advantage.

16

They interrupted Cuff and Amy in the middle of a lovely tango to tell them they were leaving. Then they enjoyed a leisurely moonlight stroll down the long driveway.

Jack kept himself between Sam and Chris the entire way to Kirby's station.

If Kirby was surprised to see Jack and Sam together, he didn't show it. He called the taxi company, then pulled his stool out of the tiny guardhouse for Chris to sit on.

"Y'all familiar with the legend of the Holy Grail?" Kirby asked her, smiling.

"I think so," she answered.

"Legend is that folks have been searching for that

precious treasure near on forever. Fighting and war-ring and praying and hunting. They think it'll bring 'em something magical."

"Eternal life, isn't it?" said Sam.

"Something along those lines." Kirby chuckled. "You know what I always wondered about that story, though?"

Chris's eyes twinkled. "What?"

"I always wondered how—and if—any of those trea-sure hunters would *recognize* it when they *found* it."

When the cab arrived, Kirby shook Sam's hand, then Jack's, and tipped his cap to Chris.

The three of them slid into the backseat; Jack made it a point to sit in the middle, which prompted a sharp look from Chris. Sam, for his part, remained remark-ably tolerant.

Jack hoped it had something to do with Sam know-ing Jack had this contest sewn up, and not seeing any use in putting up a fight.

"Where to?" the cabbie asked.

Before Jack could open his mouth, Chris gave the Jordans' address, then turned a brilliant smile toward Sam. "You and I can walk from there," she explained.

The rest of the ride was silent.

When they reached Jack's house, there were a few awkward moments in the driveway, during which Jack considered throwing Sam off his property.

It would have been easier if the guy hadn't been so decent.

"Can I use your phone?" he asked Jack. "I just want to call my folks and let them know I've had a change of plans."

"Sure," said Jack. As much as he hated the thought of letting his archrival inside his home, it would at least give him a few minutes alone with Chris. "C'mon, follow me."

"Bring me a pair of Amy's sneakers, will you, Jack?" Chris called after him. "These shoes are like torture devices."

He nodded, opening the front door for Sam.

"That way," he directed, pointing. "Past the kitchen to the family room. There's a phone on the desk in there."

"Thanks."

When Sam was gone, Jack grabbed a pair of his sister's tennis shoes out of the hall closet, then bolted back outside to Chris.

She was sitting under the huge oak tree they used to climb; the strappy high heels were already off. He tossed her the sneakers. When they were tied, she stood up.

Jack had sent Sam to the farthest phone in the house, but that still didn't leave much time. He had no choice but to hurry. She was leaning against the tree trunk, staring out toward the night sky.

Jack pressed one hand against the tree, beside her shoulder. "Nice night."

"Uh-huh." Her voice was feathery soft.

"Kind of weird being out here and not shooting hoops, huh?"

"Kinda."

They were quiet a moment; he was looking at the freckles on her nose and thinking he should have told her a long time ago how cute he thought they were.

"Chris . . ." he whispered.

At the same time, she was whispering, "Jack . . ."

He leaned in closer and noticed her quick intake of breath. Girlish. Very girlish. And sweet. She was nervous. Chris—*nervous*—for *him*. Hard to believe. He smiled.

"Jack . . ."

"Shhhh . . ." He kept leaning.

"*Jack* . . ."

He didn't let her finish; instead, he brought his hand to her chin, and as his lips touched hers, he closed his eyes.

He didn't open them again for a full three minutes.

Not because it was a great kiss or anything.

But because she'd knocked him out cold.

When Jack opened his eyes, both Chris and Sam were standing over him. Chris had her hands planted on her hips.

Things weren't looking good.

Jack raised himself until he was propped on his elbows. The movement proved to all of them that he was still alive; he had a feeling he was the only one who was glad about it.

Sam opened the bidding by letting out a long rush of breath. "I think maybe I should leave you two alone for a while."

This opinion came as something of a surprise to Jack.

Sam turned to Chris. "Look, you two have something here. I'm not sure what it is. I don't even think you're sure what it is. But it's something. I think you need to work stuff out."

"So you're going?" There was a note of sadness, maybe even pain, in her voice.

Sam must have noticed, because he smiled and reached out to brush a wisp of hair off her face. "You're not getting rid of me that easily. But I know how much you guys mean to each other. I don't want to be the reason this friendship blows up; I don't think my conscience could handle it." He laughed softly, and Jack could see Chris drinking in the sound.

"Are you mad?" she whispered.

Sam shook his head. "I'm just gonna take off, and let you two come to whatever decision it is you need to come to." He leaned over and gave her a kiss on her forehead. "I'll call you."

"Okay."

Then he shocked Jack by reaching down to shake hands. "See you around."

"Yeah," Jack murmured. "See you."

Chris watched in silence as Sam disappeared toward the street. When he was no longer visible, she glared down at Jack, who was still sprawled on the grass.

"*You* . . . are the most arrogant, ill-mannered, misguided . . ."

Jack rubbed his jaw. ". . . nitwit?"

"No, Jack. No—" She stamped three furious paces to her left, spun on her heel, then stomped the three steps back to glower above him again. "That went way beyond ordinary nitwittedness. *That* was . . . *gross!*"

"Gross?" He scambled to his feet. Anger complicated by a good dose of embarrassment flickered through him, and he narrowed his eyes.

"I can't believe you did that!"

"Well, I can't believe that you can't believe I did that!"

"Are you saying I should have expected it?" Her eyes blazed. "Are you saying I had it coming?"

"Had it coming," Jack repeated, rolling his eyes. "You make it sound like it was a good swift kick or something!"

"Maybe because that's what it felt like!" When he started to grin, she practically snarled. "That *wasn't* a compliment!"

Jack felt as if the pavement were shifting beneath his feet. He threw his arms open wide and tilted his head toward the sky. "This is crazy!" he shouted, then dragged his hands through his hair. "Didn't you want me to kiss you?"

She shook her head.

"Then"—he let out a small, frustrated choke of laughter—"then what was all that '*Jack, Jack*' garbage? Why the whispery little voice and—"

"*You* were whispering, too, you know."

"Of course I was whispering. I was getting ready to kiss you."

"And you assumed *I* was whispering because I was getting ready to be kissed?"

"Wouldn't be unheard of."

At that she marched toward him and didn't stop

until their noses were touching. "It never occurred to you that maybe I was whispering because you were standing practically on top of me? Or maybe I was whispering because it happens to be close to midnight and we're standing right underneath your little brother's bedroom window?"

Jack blinked. That hadn't, in fact, occurred to him at all. Now that she mentioned it, though, it seemed like a logical reason.

"Should have *kept* whispering" came Lukas's sleepy, disgruntled voice through the screen.

Jack ignored it. "So you didn't want me to kiss you?"

"Well, *duh*, Jack." She mimicked his arm-throwing gesture and yelled at the sky. "*No.* I didn't want you to kiss me. And you know what else?"

"What?"

"You didn't *want* to kiss me."

"Pardon?"

"You didn't."

Jack happened to disagree. He seemed to remember, prior to that sock to the chin, feeling very much as if he'd wanted to kiss her. "How do you know that?"

Chris hesitated a moment; when she answered him her voice was calmer. "Think about it, Jack. If you'd been harboring some deep, uncontrollable urge to kiss me, don't you think you would have done it a long time ago?" She gave him a curt chuckle. "I mean, it's not as if you never had the chance before."

"It was different before," Jack countered. "You were different."

"Yeah, well, that's sort of the point." Chris sighed. "You only kissed me *now* because of Sam. And because of Kyle. You thought that if they wanted to kiss me, then you should probably want to kiss me, too."

Jack watched as Chris lowered herself to the grass, wrapped her arms around her legs, and dropped her chin onto her knees. The twist in her hair had undone itself completely. He sat down next to her, careful not to make contact. She noticed, smiled.

"I'm sorry I slugged you," she said, nudging him with her shoulder.

"Yeah, well . . ." He brushed his knuckles along his jaw and grinned. "Maybe I had it coming."

They laughed together, and Jack's eyes moved to Lukas's dark window. "I'm sure Luke'll be analyzing the heck out of this one tomorrow," he predicted.

Chris shook her head. "There's nothing to analyze. You lost your mind for a minute, that's all. For a minute, you weren't thinking of me as Chris, you were thinking of me as a . . . pretty girl." She cringed self-consciously over that last part.

"Got something against pretty?" he teased.

"Only when it turns an ordinarily levelheaded guy into a maniac!"

"And what if that ordinarily levelheaded guy had been Sam?" Jack wasn't surprised to see the edges of her mouth turning up.

A brief silence passed; Chris was staring at the toes of Amy's sneakers, but Jack could feel her fidgeting beside him and knew there was more she wanted to say. Wordlessly, he stood, crossed the driveway, and picked up the basketball. The first bounce brought her head up to face him.

He held the ball aloft on his palm. It was an invitation, an olive branch, and she recognized it as one. To Jack's relief, she'd stolen the ball out of his hand and was dribbling before he even knew what hit him.

There was a lull in the rhythm of the bouncing ball as she took her first shot. *Swish.*

Together they called out "*H!*"—hers triumphant, his falsely gruff. Jack reveled in the familiarity of it.

"You know," she said, passing him the ball, "I always hated those movies where the wallflower magically blooms into a prom queen and gets the guy in the end."

Jack bounced the ball through his knees, then back again. "How come?" he asked, making his shot.

It hit the rim; Chris snatched it from under the net, then slam-dunked to earn her *O*.

"Because. It's, like, she's not supposed to care that, through the whole movie, he didn't even *know* that she was alive, just because she wore glasses or whatever. And then she ditches the glasses, or loses the braces, or undoes the braids, and all of a sudden he's madly in love with her—and she's *happy* about it, like it's some big privilege for her to turn into what *he* wants."

"Well," said Jack, recovering the ball, "you've got to admit, it's sort of how it works."

"Shouldn't work that way," she grumbled, sidestepping Jack, but not fast enough to avoid losing the ball. "And you know what's even worse? Those stories where the girl and the guy are already . . . you know . . . friends—but *just* friends—right from the beginning, but then she gets, like, this glamour makeover or something, and suddenly the guy's all over her, and they wind up"—she grabbed the ball, set it up, shot, and scored—"dating."

She leaned forward, hands on her knees, to catch her breath. "And, of course, that's what the stupid audience is hoping for all along, as if dating is supposed to be better, like it's a step-up, an improvement."

"I think I see what you mean." Jack spun the ball thoughtfully in his hands. "Like, just because she's cute now, friendship isn't good enough anymore?"

"Yeah." Chris looked up at him. "Is my mascara smearing?"

He gave her a half smile. "A little."

She wiped at her lower lashes with the back of her finger. Jack watched, unnerved by the fact that Chris looked as natural performing that action as she did oiling her baseball glove. He took a moment to let the understanding sink in.

"It's . . . it's gonna be harder to be your friend, you know, now that you look . . . like you look."

"Am I supposed to be flattered?"

Jack wasn't sure. He shrugged.

Laughing, she lunged for the ball, stole it, and swished again for the *R*. "Still dying to become one of the Beautiful People?"

He thought for a moment. "I guess not."

"Good." Chris bounced the ball and replied in a matter-of-fact tone, "Because you could never be friends with them, Jack. They may be a bunch of kids who wear the same clothes you do, and live on the same street you do. But they're different from you. From us."

"Weird, isn't it?" He let out a long sigh. "I've known them as long as I've known you."

Chris shook her head.

"What do you mean?"

"Has Dave Everett had his tonsils out?"

"What?"

"Has he?"

"I don't know."

"Have I?"

"No."

Chris nodded. "You have." She executed a flawless hook shot. "What kind of lunch box did Emily have in third grade?"

Jack shrugged.

"How about Kyle?"

"I don't think he had one. I think he just beat up other kids, and took their lunches."

"How about me?"

"That's a trick question."

"Yeah, but can you answer it?"

"Sure I can answer it. You didn't have a lunch box. You bought hot lunch every day because that was the year your mom was sick and . . ."

Chris passed the ball with a gentle bounce. "Getting the picture?"

Jack nodded, frowning. He'd told Emily she didn't know him. The fact was, he didn't really know her either. "Well, you're not totally immune either, you know. You didn't mind sharing a table with Kyle that day at the club."

She gave him a sheepish look. "Well, maybe I did think Kyle was gorgeous for, like, seven years, and maybe I gave him more credit than he deserved by thinking he was actually an interesting human being. But once I found out what a drip he is, I got over it."

"Be honest," Jack said, smiling. "It was kind of cool, having all these guys pay attention to you, watching Emily seethe."

"Yeah, it was," she admitted. "For, like, three seconds. Then it got old. I'd have rather they asked me to . . . I don't know, play tennis or something."

Jack bounced the ball and made an easy shot. "Speaking of tennis . . ."

She smiled. "Sam?"

"Yeah, Sam."

Chris grabbed the ball and held it against her hip. "Would you mind if we talked about Sam tomorrow?"

"Deal." Jack lunged forward, stole the ball, and made a three-point shot. "Maybe we'll talk about . . ."

"Kara?"

"Yeah. Kara. Maybe we'll talk about Kara, tomorrow, too."

Then the square of Lukas's window went golden with light, and they could see his small silhouette against the screen, watching.

A breeze came up, and the moths fluttered like confetti around the garage light; the crickets seemed to urge them on as they played, challenging and cheering each other, long into the night.